*I think it is possible for ordinary people
to choose to be extraordinary.*

—Elon Musk

Chapter 1
THE RACE

Carson Lox's palms were sweaty as he nudged the throttle forward. The ViperLyte FPV racing quadrotor drone responded instantly, nudging towards eighty miles per hour.

His craft banked effortlessly between the track's neon-blue signs, which became high-speed blurs as he zoomed past. Ahead, the running lights of Logan46 blinked their silent challenge at him.

"Come on!" Carson howled. He gritted his teeth in concentration as Logan46 abruptly shot straight up to avoid a sheer wall in their path. Carson heaved the joysticks back and followed the leader in a steep climb – but it was a short one. A vast dark ceiling filled his view and he heard the plastic on his radio controller creak as he pushed the sticks forward to level his aircraft out.

Had he been a split second slower, he would have hit the ceiling at full pelt. There would be no coming back from that. It would have meant death in a shower of plastic pieces.

Concentrate, he silently ordered himself as he drew closer to Logan46. His rival may have had superior engines able to spin him through tight circles, but Carson's drone had been tricked out by his engineer and he knew he was faster. And now the racers were on a straight, he had the advantage.

The track strobed its multicoloured yellow and red stripes beneath him, and the noise from the crowd began to rise as he doggedly pursued his rival.

Ahead, a flashing circle indicated the descent into hell – a fully enclosed tube that coiled like a snake. Most pilots would be forced to slow down here, but not Carson. And clearly not Logan46.

The view ahead was suddenly swamped by darkness as they plummeted at speed into the tunnel. The speedometer floating over his display clicked over ... 89 ... 90. Only the drones' headlights revealed the curving walls that spiralled down and to the right.

Carson's jaw began to cramp – he was clenching his teeth out of sheer concentration. He had memorized the course; every twist and turn...

Logan46 suddenly slowed as it performed a barrel roll right in front of Carson. It was a pointless display of acrobatics – but it had the desired effect.

Carson nudged the controls to the left to avoid colliding – but he was going too fast to compensate for the abrupt turn in the tunnel. The edge of his forward portside rotors clipped the wall and shattered. The aircraft lurched to the left under the strain of the missing propeller and Carson's aircraft spun one hundred and eighty degrees around—

Just in time to see the racer in third place behind him round the tunnel bend and slam into him at full speed.

Carson's world went black.

Carson yanked his virtual reality headset off in anger. He rubbed his sore hazel eyes as they adjusted from the FPV (first person view) of the goggles and looked out over the course that was spread over three levels of the multistorey car park. The crowd whooped as Logan46 crossed the finishing line in record time.

Logan himself stood several metres away, his radio control unit firmly in his hands as his fingers nudged the sticks to make his drone perform a victory roll around them. Sweat poured around his VR glasses, which were covered in stickers: a skull and crossbones and another declaring him to be *King of the Sky*. His crew of three long-haired, muscular teens stood behind, swapping high fives. One looked at Carson and spread his index finger and thumb across his forehead: *loser*.

"Smooth move," said Eddie from behind. He was three centimetres smaller, quite a few wider, and a month younger than Carson. All twelve years old, Carson's team were the youngest racers here. Eddie (his full name *Edward*, every letter pronounced by his parents when he was in trouble) wore thick glasses, permanently marred by greasy fingerprints, that he always joked were AR goggles – *actual reality*. He was, for want of any better position, the team manager.

"That was a dirty trick," Carson growled, slamming his visor on to the table.

Eddie hissed and scooped it up as if it were made of glass instead of plastic. He stroked the headset protectively. "Easy with those! You don't have to break *everything*!"

"Well, Team Logan are known for their dirty tricks, Carson," said Trix – again, not her real name, but she *hated* Tracy, even when she was in a good mood. Her dark brown skin was covered in sweat due to the humidity in the car park. It was so bad that her hair, normally gelled straight up in a cool spike – or a brush, as Eddie liked to tease – was already threatening to wilt like a badly watered yucca plant. "And I think you trashed my engine at the very least," she reminded him. As the team's official engineer, she traditionally complained about the slightest scratch on their drone. From the quiet way she spoke this time, Carson and Eddie were left in no doubt that she was saving her yelling voice for later.

"I really thought we could have won..." Eddie sighed. "Even second place. I could have done with the money."

They all could have. They had begged and borrowed to build their latest drone, and Carson knew that it would be a long time before they could afford to fix a broken engine. If there was any further damage to the drone – and after a ninety-miles-per-hour crash, that was likely – then they would be well and truly stuffed.

"Carsonators?" came a voice from behind. Carson turned in recognition of their team name – and immediately regretted it.

Three bigger kids scowled at them. They all wore matching black tank tops with a familiar AirBlitz logo. The very same logo on the drone Carson had just flown into. Their pilot's VR headset hung from his neck, and the radio controller in his hand had chunks of plastic missing from it where he had presumably slammed it frustration.

The furious spotty drone pilot tilted his head until his neck cracked. Then he thrust a fat finger into Carson's ribs.

"You sabotaged my race! You owe me a new drone," he said menacingly.

Chapter 2
HIGH COMMAND

General Lewis's arm automatically saluted as he passed more air force personnel on his way up the steep staircase. The steps ended at a platform that opened up in the fresh air, and the general found himself standing at the top of a tall, empty grandstand perched on a grassy hill. It overlooked a town – or rather, a fake town. The buildings were plain wooden structures but had real windows and doorways, some decorated with blinds and curtains.

It reminded the general of the models he used to make out of old cereal packets when he was a lad, except this one even had self-driving vehicles lining the streets and mannequins poised as commuters and families.

"We call it Summersville."

The voice from behind him caused General Lewis to flinch in surprise. The speaker was Jira Zushi, a small Indian man wearing a smart blue suit with a crisp white T-shirt underneath. His wiry beard clung desperately to his chin in a fashion Lewis had heard called *hipster*, but he could be wrong; fashion wasn't something the air force was ever involved with. Jira looked every inch the brilliant technology billionaire he was.

"I think our engineers had a little too much fun setting it up," Jira sighed as he gestured to one dummy walking a plastic dog. "But you get the idea. It's a regular town."

"I was told this was a demonstration for a new peacekeeping initiative," General Lewis said in a bored tone. He went to many displays of new technology and weapons, and none were ever as good as promised.

"Indeed." Jira rubbed his hands together eagerly. "All around the world, police forces are overstretched, as are military operations, as you well know. More troops are needed after a war to keep the peace than required during it."

Lewis nodded impatiently. He was aware of the problem.

"What if I can take all that hassle away from you? What if we could make the streets, not just of troubled countries but of our very own, safe for everybody?"

Lewis opened his mouth to reply but stopped when he saw the gleam in Jira's eyes. Jira extended his hand like a showman revealing his circus's biggest act.

"I bring you, the Vanta Hawk!"

A small aircraft suddenly shot into view and orbited the test range. Lewis strained to listen, but he couldn't hear any noise from the engines. Even a drone usually gave a telltale buzz.

Jira watched him closely. "It has revolutionary electric engines boosted by solar power that increases range and makes it stealthily quiet. The fuselage has *very special* capabilities. And is made from graphene and vanta arrays."

The general raised his hand to silence him. "I'll read the sales brochure later. Show me what it can do."

The Vanta Hawk weaved between the buildings at high speed before banking around and heading straight for the grandstand. Lewis expected it to zoom low overhead – instead it hurtled straight at them. He tensed, ready to jump aside – but the Vanta Hawk stopped dead and silently hovered.

Despite himself, the general was impressed. Against the clear blue sky it was difficult to judge how big the drone was. He noticed the rotors were held on upward-arcing arms and twitched precisely to maintain the aircraft's balance in the light breeze. He still couldn't hear anything from the electric engines. A large transparent orb sat on its tail, reminding him of a glow-worm as green and blue lights flashed within.

"That's one heck of a quadcopter." As soon as he saw Jira's smile broaden, he added, "But we have plenty of those in the air force." He had expected Jira's smile to vanish. Instead, it grew.

"Not like this you haven't. You see, General, there is no pilot. There is no person at the controls, neither here nor halfway around the globe." It was common practice for military drones to be piloted from bases deep in the English countryside, while they were flying in cities on the opposite side of the planet. "The AG-421 Vanta Hawk is the very latest in artificial intelligence."

"You mean, that thing is controlling *itself*?"

"I mean, she *thinks* for herself." Jira indicated to the pulsing orb as tiny lights flickered through it like a glitter storm. "That is her brain. An advanced artificial brain that enables her to reason on her own. We can even download her personality and transfer it if needed." He turned to face the drone, and General Lewis was surprised to see the aircraft pivot around to face him. "Good morning, AG-421."

A camera the size of a large mug swivelled between the two men, as if studying them. The general could see his own reflection in the large lens. Then, to his surprise, a perfectly synthesized woman's voice answered.

"Good morning, sir."

Jira gestured to the general. "This is General Lewis from the air force. He has come a long way to see what you can do."

Lewis was rendered speechless when the drone turned to face him.

"Good morning, General. I'm looking forward to putting on a show for you today."

Jira's eyes darted between Lewis and the drone as he spoke: "Then please show the good general what you are capable of. I believe there is a bank robbery in progress. The thieves are heading to their getaway car and have the manager as hostage. Stop them."

The drone immediately pulled backwards and climbed high into the air. General Lewis watched open-mouthed as Jira began a running commentary.

"AG-421 has a wide range of sensors on-board. She is climbing to get a full view of the town so she can assess where the threat is. To make things more difficult we have built three banks below, so she doesn't know which one is being robbed."

The sound of an alarm bell suddenly echoed through the streets.

"Ah, now she does. Based on evidence, she can work out the most likely target."

The Vanta Hawk immediately changed course and plummeted towards the ground like a bird of prey.

"We have a real getaway car. Radio controlled by one of my team."

On cue, a blue hatchback parked in front of the bank pulled away at speed, joining the flow of automated cars, just as the drone soared over it. Lewis blinked in surprise as the drone came to a rapid halt and spun in a tight U-turn to chase the car.

The getaway car skidded wide across a junction, forcing the driverless cars to screech to a halt. The hatchback sped up a side street, weaving between traffic to avoid pursuit, but high in the air the drone fell in behind it. No matter what agile driving the human operator did, the Vanta Hawk stayed on its tail.

"And now the drone's party trick. She's fully armed." As Jira spoke, General Lewis saw a small weapons pod lower from beneath the craft's belly. "We have an innocent hostage on-board but need to stop the car before it causes an accident. AG-421 will assess the situation and dangers, and then—"

Before he could finish there was a flash of light from the drone's belly and a puff of smoke. A missile raced the short distance to the car and blew off a rear wheel. The car rocked violently, threatening to tip over before it skidded across a junction with smoke pouring from the wheel arch. With a loud bang, it slammed to a halt against a school bus that had been turning left. Vanta Hawk swooped in and hovered menacingly over the getaway car, but again the distance made it impossible to judge the drone's size.

Jira cleared his throat, a little embarrassed by the destruction. "Minimal damage and the hostage will be alive and well."

Flames suddenly licked across the back of the car and in seconds the rear half was ablaze. General Lewis glanced at Jira.

"Minimal damage?"

Jira shifted uncomfortably. "In reality, the thieves would have been out of the car already."

"And those on the bus?"

Jira hesitated before answering. "Maybe a few cuts and bruises, but nothing too serious."

With a powerful boom, the petrol tank on the getaway car exploded as the flames reached it. The entire car flipped up – then came crashing down on top of the bus. Lewis arched a questioning eyebrow at Jira.

Jira already had his phone in hand and continued the presentation as if nothing had happened. "And the Vanta Hawk can intercept any communications, allowing it to assess potential problems. For example, it now thinks I am calling the police." He dialled a fake number and spoke. "We have a terrorist situation! Red shirts have taken prisoners in several buildings. We need help!"

General Lewis's eye darted to one of the tower block windows. He had caught a glimpse of red inside earlier but thought nothing of it. Now he looked again he could see a mannequin in a red shirt wielding a gun. He soon noticed others scattered in several buildings. When he looked back, the aircraft was already on the move.

Jira narrated. "AG-421 is capable of making instant decisions without the need for a human operator to intervene."

As he spoke, the drone arced around to the red-shirted dummy the general had spotted. Another missile was shot through the window and both men watched with open mouths as the entire top of the tower exploded in a huge mushroom cloud. By the time the black smoke had thinned enough, General Lewis saw the drone had looped over the town and smashed through the window of another building. It rammed through several rooms at speed, smashing apart the plasterboard walls before colliding with another red shirt, which was destroyed from the impact. Then the drone punctured the far wall like a high-speed wrecking ball. A second later the two floors above collapsed with a loud crash.

The Vanta Hawk came to a stop, hovering near the grandstand.

"Mission accomplished," said the calm voice.

General Lewis's mouth hung slack in astonishment. He slowly turned to Jira, who gave a small shrug.

"There are maybe *one or two* teething problems..."

Chapter 3
HOME

"A thousand quid down the toilet," sighed Trix as her soldering iron sizzled a wire which she pulled free. She sat at Carson's desk, sleeves of her top rolled to the elbows, his table lamp poised overhead to illuminate the twisted drone's chassis.

Carson sat on his bed, surrounded by a mixture of posters from his favourite bands, sleek stealth aircraft poised against the clouds, and several drone racing championship ads he had printed from the internet. He rubbed his black eye, a present from the AirBlitz team, who apparently didn't like younger kids answering back. That had been almost a week ago, and it was only just fading.

"There's this new National League event next month." He blew strands of his overly long black hair from his eyes as he tugged a poster from the wall and flapped it to get their attention. "The Constructor League. Online it said any drone can race. They can all be different."

Proper leagues had strict rules to ensure all the drones had the same specs, like Formula One racing, to make sure the racers were evenly matched.

"Ours is definitely different," Eddie said, without looking up from the game he was playing on his tablet. "It can't fly."

Carson tapped the poster. "Look, it's got a thousand-pound prize! We'd be rich!"

Eddie finally looked up as his game abruptly ended. "Well, one, we didn't even finish the Carpark League race. Two, we no longer have a drone to enter with."

Carson jumped from his bed and crossed to Trix. "Are you kidding? Trix'll have this flying in no time."

Trix cracked open the drone's plastic body. It had caught fire during the collision, melting the case like cheese on to most of the circuits inside. She used her fingers to pry a board free. Instead of the familiar green, it was as black as a piece of overcooked toast.

"Not this time." She tossed it to him. Carson tried to catch it, but it bounced from his palm to the floor. "The circuits are fried. The propellers have all shattered. Two of the three remaining motors are burned out. On the other hand, the RC receiver may be salvageable, and the camera still works."

Carson nudged the blackened circuit board with the toe of his battered Converse trainer, then stared at the table on which Trix had dismantled their drone like a surgeon, a skill he reckoned she'd inherited from her dad, who really was one. He picked up the camera lens, half the size of his little fingernail. It still had the ribbon cable dangling from it.

"So, this is all the drone we have left working?"

"Yeah, although I'm not *entirely* sure that it works." Her dark eyes sparkled mischievously. "I was just trying to cheer you up. I need my laptop to check it. If you want me to be brutally honest, I think our drone racing days are over. The Carsonators are dead."

"Stupid team name anyway," mumbled Eddie

as he inched his glasses up to rub his eyes before restarting his game.

Carson put the camera back on the desk. "We'll build a new one."

Eddie peeked at them over his tablet. "Do you have a magic box of spare parts?"

"No. But we must have *some*. . .?"

Trix grabbed her backpack off the floor. "Not any more. We used most of them after Eddie flew into a wall."

"How was I supposed to see that?"

"It was the side of a *warehouse*. It had always been there, Edward." She ignored his scowl. "Then we had that race in the sports hall when the engine-management system burnt itself out. The other one on that sports weekend when you clipped two rotors on a tree. And we used the last spares in tonight's race. Besides, they were all spare *parts* – not a spare drone."

"And do we have any money?" His hand went to his jeans pocket and found a single pound coin hiding there.

"Zero!" Trix nudged Carson. "We could ask your dad."

Carson looked away, and smoothed his floppy

hair back from his eyes. He didn't really talk to his dad. The very idea of asking him for *anything* was unthinkable. Not that it mattered. His dad was seldom at home and he wouldn't understand that drone racing was a legitimate, cutting-edge sport. Carson knew his dad wouldn't understand how exciting it was flying through obstacle courses at high speeds against others. And when flown through a pair of virtual reality goggles, Carson felt as if he was flying like Superman.

Flying...

The freedom, the adrenaline, the thrills ... he couldn't think of any other sport like it.

Trix patted him on the shoulder. "Well, it was good while it lasted." She opened the door to leave.

"Wait!" Carson picked up the wrecked ViperLyte and turned it in his hand to examine it from every angle. "What if we build another one?"

Trix rolled her eyes. "Duh. We've just been through that. We have no spare parts or money to buy anything."

Carson wagged the drone at her. "No. I mean build another one from *scratch*, with parts not meant for drones. Bigger, better, faster than ever before."

The comment distracted Eddie enough for him to lose his last life. He lowered the tablet and frowned at Carson. "Is that possible?"

Carson shrugged and they both turned to Trix, who hesitated by the door. "Well ... I *suppose* it is. But where would we get the parts from?"

"The scrapyard just off the bypass. I've seen bits of old planes in there from the local airfield. There must be tons of cool things we can use."

Eddie and Trix burst into laughter. Eddie shook his head.

"You think we can just walk in there and buy them with our invisible money? Unless you mean stealing them?" He laughed again ... then stopped when he saw the earnest look on Carson's face. "We can't nick them! That's not right!"

"It's just scrap!" Carson insisted as he put the battered drone down. "Where's the harm? It's not like it's being used. And after we win, we'll pay for whatever we took." He saw the doubt in their faces. "Come on, it's the middle of the summer. Do you want to go the rest of the holidays without a single race? Do you want to give it all up when we're this close —" he held up a thumb and forefinger millimetres apart "– to victory? We're a good team. We deserve a shot."

The silence in the room became thicker. Finally, Trix spoke up.

"You want us to risk life and limb to break into a scrapyard. Steal stuff to make our own drone from *nothing*, just so we can enter a race?"

Carson nodded.

"That sounds like the most stupid plan I have ever heard."

Carson grinned. "Yeah. But wouldn't it be fun?"

Chapter 4
SCRAPYARD CHALLENGE

"The secret is not to *show* you're afraid!"

That was all right for Eddie to say, thought Carson, but he wasn't the one balanced on a wobbly chain-link fence with a snarling Dobermann pacing on the other side, looking like it hadn't eaten all summer. His heart was pounding in his chest.

"You can always jump back down?" suggested Trix as she eyed the drooling dog. She had yet to dismount her bicycle since they had arrived. Her foot was still on the raised pedal, ready for a fast getaway.

Carson didn't need convincing, but his legs felt like jelly and he was unable to move.

"I know, I'll distract him with a stick," Eddie said, shining his torch on the ground around him. He slackened his hoodie so he could better move his head. In a desperate attempt to conceal his face, he'd pulled the hood so tight that only his glasses poked out like some kind of cheap space monster. "Then you just jump down. He won't bother you."

"How do you know that?"

"I'm a dog person. Dog people know these things." Eddie found a crooked stick and, without pause, lobbed it over the fence. "Fetch!"

Carson took a deep breath and dropped down into the scrapyard. Only when he was mid-air did he realize the dog hadn't chased the stick. With a bored expression, it had merely watched it vanish into the darkness.

He landed in a crouch that knocked the breath from him, but his legs were already moving, propelling him forward. Behind, he heard claws scrabble on the concrete and the dog's wild barking.

He heard both Trix and Eddie yell behind him. "Run!"

Carson sprinted as fast as he was able, with his torch pointed ahead like a sword slicing through the darkness. The black shadows of cars, a boat, old cookers and even fragments of tails and wings from old aircraft and other twisted metallic relics formed a towering canyon, forcing him down an aisle of mud. He splashed through puddles, his feet slipping.

His heart was pounding so hard, Carson was afraid it would break a rib. As the scurry of claws on the ground drew closer, his legs turned to jelly. Blood pounded in his ears, blotting out any other sound. Now not hearing the dog was somehow more terrifying, as if it had turned into a stealth dog. Was it still behind him? He dared not look.

Then something nudged his bum and he guessed the animal had just tried to take a silent bite from him. Fearing his legs were about to give in, Carson sharply changed direction. He sprang to the side, landing on a sheet of metal which buckled and – with a pop – catapulted him a little into the air. He hadn't been prepared for the boost and his arms and legs flailed uselessly. And with it, he lost his grip on the torch – and could only watch it sail into the junk.

Carson landed on the bonnet of a rusting car just in time to see the last light of his torch vanish in a crevasse of trash. Then the world around him was plunged into darkness. A waning moon provided just enough light to make out the jagged peaks of the rubbish piles against the grey clouds, but that was about it. Beneath him the Dobermann broke its silence and woofed furiously at him. He could hear claws scrabbling against metal, followed by a whimper as the mutt slid back down.

Any relief Carson felt for not being mauled to death vanished when he realized he was stuck on top of a heap of junk in the dark. Then it started to rain.

"I've lost my torch!" Carson called out. "I'm stuck!"

Surely his friends could still hear him; he hadn't run for very long, had he? But if they could, he couldn't hear their reply over the increasing rain that plinked and plonked from the metal hill, and the Dobermann's steady barking.

"Hello?" His voice reverberated in the steel canyon. "I'm stuck! Help!"

...*Elp* ... *elp* ... *elp*... came the echo.

A distinct BEE-BOP caught his attention. He turned sharply around, trying to trace where the sound had come from. It was electronic, like an old walkie-talkie bleep, or the battery warning from a phone. Carson wondered if a security guard had been watching his dog encounter all along and was now attempting to sneak up on him.

"Hello?" he said, a little louder.

BEE-BOP!

This time he saw a flicker of light from amongst the junk further up the pile. Perhaps somebody had lost a mobile phone? He scrambled over, shards of metal bruising his shins and arms. If he wasn't careful he imagined tumbling backwards down the hill and being impaled on a jagged spear of wreckage or falling on to a razor-sharp sheet of metal that could chop his head off.

He reached the spot where he thought he'd seen the light. The sound of rain drowned almost everything out . . . except the dog.

"Hello?" he tried again.

He was answered by a flicker of light and the beeping tone from a hole in the junk near his feet. The flash left an imprint on his eye like a camera flash, but it was enough to see the circular hole was about the size of a car and he was centimetres from blundering into it in the dark. He knelt at the edge and peered down. Water was pooling on the compacted junk, forming tiny waterfalls that plunged into the pit.

"Beep if you're there – aaaarrrrghhh!"

The lip of the hole gave way under Carson's hands and he was sent tumbling head first into the pit. In the darkness he had no sense of which way was up, but received a solid answer seconds later. . .

Chapter 5
THE DISCOVERY

Carson hit several objects on the way down. Each smashed apart under his weight, but at least they slowed his descent enough so that when he landed on his back, only the breath was knocked from him. A large sheet of metal buckled under his weight, but it broke his fall. He gasped for breath as he sat up, noting that he had landed on the side of a large, rusting water tank. Then he realized he could see; everything was now bathed in a harsh blue light that came from under a pile of metal panels that had fallen in with him.

He was in a cave amongst the junk. Water

trickled in above him, cascading down walls lined with crumpled washing machines, industrial tubes, pipes and car grills that resembled grinning faces. He wondered if he could climb out, but it was at least seven metres to the top, and the ceiling curved inwards, making the exit hole inaccessible.

He was trapped.

Carson forced himself to remain calm. Panicking would achieve nothing. He rolled from the water tank, splashing into a puddle that was rapidly forming at his feet. *Great*, he thought, *maybe I'll drown before I starve to death.*

With a grunt he lifted one of the panels. It was interlocked with the others, so in moving one, the others slid away with a clatter that was deafening in the cave. Then the light flared brighter, forcing him to turn away and shield his eyes. When he risked a peek, he saw the illumination had dimmed considerably. He remained motionless to let his eyes adjust to the darkness, hearing nothing more than the sound of his own breathing and the trickling rain.

Stay calm. . .

He blinked a few times and could finally make

out more details in the gloom. The light was still there, just fainter and steadily pulsing as if breathing. It came from a sphere about the size of a golf ball. The glass surface was covered in a network of lines that appeared to connect randomly pulsing points of light. Carson moved closer for a better look, and only then realized the orb was attached to something. To his astonishment, he realized it was a small drone, no bigger than a hard-backed book.

"Wow!" he said aloud. The sound seemed enough to trigger a BEE-BOP and a wave of light rippled through the orb, rapidly changing into a kaleidoscope of colours as it did so. The body of the drone was streamlined like a prime racer and its propellers sat on two pairs of arms that gracefully arced upwards.

"You're incredible!" He dropped to his knees for a closer look. "I mean, you're exactly what I'm looking for. Which is all kinds of weird." He stopped and looked around, half expecting his friends to step out and declare it was all some stupid stunt for YouTube.

Nobody appeared. He turned his attention back to the drone.

"I guess today's my lucky day. I mean, if I was

looking for an old fridge or washing machine –"
he gestured to the junk around him "– then I'd be
super lucky. Instead . . . here I am with you. Talking
to myself." He rubbed his head, wondering if he
wasn't in fact imagining all of this and was instead
lying unconscious in a puddle. He pinched himself
to check.

"Ow!" That proved he was awake. Unless, of
course, he had imagined the pain too.

Carson could see debris had fallen into the
blades. One even had a snarl of electrical wire
knotted in it. He ran his hand along the dirty, wet
bodywork. Whatever the material was underneath
felt soft and warm. It wasn't metal nor plastic, and
he could swear it rippled under his fingertips. At
the front of the machine was a camera the size of a
bottle top. It was angled to face the floor and mud
had splattered the lens. It was the sorriest-looking
aircraft he had ever seen.

"Aren't you a mess?" He wiped the mud off the
camera with the only part of his sleeve that was dry.
Then he plucked out the rubbish that had fallen
between the propeller blades.

"Who would throw you away?" he said quietly

as he set about unthreading the wire from the rear blades. He pulled the last of it free with a hard yank that set the propeller free-spinning for a few moments. "I suppose we're both trapped down here."

He wondered where his friends were. Surely they would look for him when he didn't return?

Knowing Eddie, he'd probably gone home when it started raining.

Fighting rising panic, Carson stood and tilted his head upwards. The rain was increasing at an alarming rate. He cupped his hands around his mouth and bellowed.

"Can anybody hear me? I'm stuck!"

He strained hard for any response. Maybe his friends had gone to fetch help? He couldn't even hear the guard dog. He glanced at the drone, realizing it too had stopped making any sounds. Other than the flickering orb, it was utterly dead.

"I suppose your batteries are almost out," he sighed as he approached the wall of junk. "Looks like I'm going to have to save myself."

He used the wire to form a loop around one of the drone's wing-arms and fastened the other end to his jeans' belt loop. Then he began to climb. The first few steps were easy. The mangled wrecks provided easy footholds. However, his hands stung as jagged metal cut into them.

With a hiss of pain, Carson slipped and fell back down on to the muddy wet ground, and his head banged against something hard. Almost immediately his vision began to swim. He groped the back of his head and found he was bleeding.

"Oh, no. . ." The words slurred from his mouth. He tried to stand but his wobbly legs dropped him back down. "Help. . ." The word was no more than a whisper as he fought to stay conscious despite the rain pouring across his face.

Carson wasn't entirely sure what happened next.

A rising whine echoed through the cave, then everything became silent. Even the rain stopped and was replaced with a constant blast of air from above. He forced his eyes open and saw something hanging just above his head. Thinking a saviour had lowered something to enable him to climb out, he reached for it. His cut hands stung as something looped around his wrist and pulled tight. The very next moment he was plucked into the air at high speed.

"WWWHHOOOAA!!"

It felt as if he was flying, but a nagging voice at the back of his mind assured him he was lying dazed in the junk cave.

Still, it was a very detailed hallucination.

He looked straight down as his soggy trainers pedalled nothing but air as the mountains of scrap passed centimetres below. He looked up in time to see the hulk of a crashed lorry rush towards him.

"AARGH!"

At the very last second he veered aside, so close to pancaking into the cab that he heard the whoosh as he passed by. Then his stomach lurched as he dropped towards the muddy avenue. He was losing consciousness now, knowing this wasn't real. In the distance he heard the very angry Dobermann resume its chase.

He forced his eyes open and was surprised to see he was now rushing towards the fence. He decided the world was less confusing with his eyes closed.

"Are you OK?" Trix asked with concern.

Carson flicked his eyes open and was puzzled to discover he really was lying on the other side of the fence. The Dobermann was clawing at the chain-link and barking itself into a froth. Carson pushed himself upright. "I think so."

Trix's wet hair was plastered to her face as she looked between Carson and the fence. "How did you get over the fence?"

"I just made it . . . I think the drone lifted me out."

Trix and Eddie exchanged a puzzled look. Eddie wiped raindrops from his glasses and knelt down to retrieve the small drone that lay on its side in the mud next to Carson.

"You mean this little thing?"

When Carson nodded, it felt as if his brain was loose in his skull. "Yeah. But . . . it's small."

Eddie's grin slowly melted away as he looked at Trix again. "Mate, I think you banged your head." He stood up and examined the drone. "I mean, this is a wicked find, but you're no Mary Poppins." He held the drone up like Poppins' umbrella. "It didn't just hop you into the air."

Carson touched the back of his head. He hissed with pain. When he brought his hand back to see, Trix's torch illuminated blood on his fingers.

"You really did bang your head!" Eddie exclaimed in horror.

Whatever he said next, Carson didn't hear, as the world around him faded away and he blacked out.

Chapter 6

GROUNDED

Carson had only passed out again for a few seconds, but it had been enough for his friends to decide to get him to the hospital, ASAP.

Especially because he was babbling about the drone flying him over the scrapyard.

Eddie shoved the small drone into Carson's backpack and patted him on the arm. "It'd be a miracle if you had any brain to damage, mate. But we better check."

They sat him on his bike, and Trix, being the tallest, walked with it, while Eddie shoved the other two bikes along. Fortunately, A&E was only a mile away, just past the old derelict cinema that still had faded posters up for movies half a decade old. They were soaked to the skin by the time they reached it. Before stepping into the hospital, they decided it would be wise to avoid mentioning that they broke into the scrapyard and so created a cover story about falling off a swing in the local playground.

They also agreed not to tell Carson's dad.

The first thing the nurses did was inject him with a tetanus shot before giving him a few stitches on the cut at the back of his head. After an X-ray, the doctor declared it was nothing more than a mild bump. Carson fingered his stiches, proud of his impressive wound, but less so when his dad turned up after the nurses had immediately contacted him.

"What did I tell you about playing around on those swings? They're a deathtrap!"

Carson rubbed his head and avoided looking his father in the eye as he rolled his bike to the car. "I'm fine. Thanks for asking."

"I know how you are. The doctor's told me nothing was broken and that thick skull of yours is in one piece." He hesitated, searching for the right words. "Otherwise . . . I might have been worried." He lifted Carson's bike on to the roof rack. "But getting a call like that when I'm at work. . ."

Carson opened the car door and climbed inside. "I didn't ask them to call you," he muttered, slamming the door closed.

His dad opened his mouth as if to argue, but instead only a low, sad sigh came out. He nodded to Trix and Eddie, just about managing a whispered *thank you*, before he climbed in the car too. He slid the key into the ignition but didn't turn it. Instead he and Carson listened to increasing rain drumming the vehicle.

"Carson, you can't take risks. I can't afford to lose. . ." He stopped himself and took a deep breath. "If I can't trust you while I'm working—"

"You'll what? Ground me?" Carson immediately regretted sounding so harsh, but the words were out. He glanced sidelong at his dad and couldn't help but think he was looking thinner than usual, his hair a little greyer than last summer, and the dark bags under his eyes told Carson that he was getting the bare minimum of sleep, just like him.

His dad's voice softened. It almost sounded as

if he was upset. "OK, fine. You're grounded for the rest of the week."

It was a threat Carson had heard many times, but without his father being home much, it was impossible to enforce. Carson knew it wasn't worth arguing. He sat in the car, clutching the backpack on his knees while his father tried to start the car. He stared defiantly straight ahead as the vehicle shuddered to life on the third attempt.

The only sound on the way home was the screech of torn window wipers attempting to clear the driving rain. His father turned on the radio and didn't ask any further questions.

Carson went straight to his room and closed the door. He felt like slamming it to annoy his dad, but the last thing he wanted was another pointless confrontation. He quickly towelled his hair dry, changed out of his wet clothes, and put on a baggy Blue Jays baseball top he'd once bought on a holiday in Toronto and a pair of grey tracksuit bottoms. Then he pulled his phone out, shoved the backpack in his wardrobe and lay on his bed to message his friends.

After ten minutes he heard the front door close,

followed by the croak of the car engine turning over. Carson listened as the vehicle pulled away, then he leapt from the bed and retrieved his backpack from the wardrobe.

He carefully slid the drone from the backpack and placed it on his desk. He angled his table light to get a better look. The fuselage was a creamy white, with a blue stripe along both sides. The texture felt warm to the touch, and when he ran his finger along it, it felt like smooth scales, similar to a snake he had once handled in a petting zoo.

"How'd you get me out?" he whispered.

The drone failed to answer. The spherical orb that had lit up the cave was completely dark. He gently tapped it, hoping for a sign of life, but it remained off. For a moment he considered opening it up to tinker with the battery, but decided he'd only succeed in breaking it. Trix was far more qualified at fixing things.

Instead, Carson drew up his chair to the desk and rested his chin on his folded arms as he peered at the drone. It was obviously impossible that it had lifted him out... In fact, perhaps he had climbed from the cave and over the fence on his own? But after hitting his head the moment had been wiped from his memory?

Trix and Eddie certainly hadn't seen him clamber, or even fly, over the fence. They had only been alerted to his escape when the dog ran against the chain-link, barking louder than ever.

He touched the scar on the back of his head. No, the bump had caused him to imagine his grand escape. The more he convinced himself that's what happened, the more it made sense.

"Either that or I'm losing my mind," he whispered aloud. "Imagine that. Waking up and finding out you're somebody else. Or you've forgotten everything."

Part of him longed for that. Being able to forget.

He gently blew on one of the quadcopter's propellers. It easily spun around. "You're making me go bonkers."

He picked up the drone and used a cloth to gently polish its oversized camera lens. He was so engrossed that he almost jumped from his skin when there was a loud and persistent knocking downstairs.

*

Trix had arrived with her tool belt. She'd taken time to change her T-shirt to something with Ninja Hamsters on it, and her damp hair was now flattened in a sort-of pixie cut that made her look smarter. Eddie still wore his wet hoodie, but came armed with a bag of chocolate and crisps he had found carelessly lying in his sister's room. They were both out of breath after furiously pedalling over. Their bikes lay discarded in the drive as they thundered upstairs to examine the booty Carson had found.

"Well, it *looks* cool," Eddie said, cramming a whole chocolate bar in his mouth. "But did you find a radio controller too?"

"I was sort of busy fighting a tribe of wild junk warriors defending the wasteland."

Eddie nudged the craft, leaving a chocolatey fingerprint on it. "It looks a bit too small to fly you through the scrapyard," he tittered.

"Shut up, *Edward*!" Carson grumbled.

Eddie dropped back in his chair, pulling a face. "No need to be rude," he muttered.

Trix unrolled her tool belt, revealing an assortment of tools that included tiny spanners, wrenches, screwdrivers, a soldering iron and a multimeter. She selected a Torx screwdriver and carefully picked the drone up, turning it around as she searched for a way to open it.

"It looks new. Camera lens isn't smashed, can't see any cracks, and the props aren't broken either."

"Open it up and see if you can replace the battery," said Carson. He was feeling impatient just to see the drone light up again.

Trix's reply was nothing more than a long, low, "Mmmm..." After almost a minute of scrutinizing the drone up close, she spoke again. "That might be tricky."

"Why?"

"There aren't any screws." She held it upside down to show the boys. She tapped the casing with the screwdriver. "This is so well put together they're all probably hidden under it." She rubbed her finger along the fuselage. "And I'm not even sure this is plastic. Feels odd. Maybe carbon fibre? Or something else..."

"Can't you just pop it off?" asked Eddie.

"I could, if I knew how it came apart." Trix gently tried to move the edges of the protective casing but it didn't budge. "If I pull too hard I might break something." She gently placed the drone down on the desk and turned to Carson. "Check on your iPad for any others like this." She sat on the bed next to him so she could see the screen. "There may be instructions on how to open it."

A loud thud from behind made Carson and Trix whirl around. Eddie stood over the desk looking guilty. In his hand he held a small hammer from Trix's belt.

"What are you doing?" screamed Carson. He darted over and snatched the hammer from Eddie's grasp.

"I thought I'd try and crack the case open!"

"You idiot!" huffed Trix as she joined them. "You've probably broken the electrics inside!"

"I doubt it. I didn't even scratch it!" Eddie pointed to the case. Sure enough, there wasn't a mark on it. "And I hit it hard. See?"

Without pausing, he snatched the hammer back from Carson and slammed it against the drone.

This time both Carson and Trix grabbed Eddie's arms and pulled him back.

"Stop it!" Carson snapped.

Trix took back her hammer. "Don't touch my stuff!"

"But look!" Eddie said, nodding towards the drone. There was no sign of impact. They had crashed enough drones to have seen protective cases smash apart.

The orb on the back of the drone suddenly lit up, spilling bright neon-blue light across the room. But only for a few seconds before fading.

"What did you do?" Trix snapped.

"Nothing!" Eddie exclaimed.

"It still has a little juice left." Trix fished a charging pack from her pack. She plugged it into the wall and held the small pad that usually clipped to the battery. "There must be a power port somewhere..."

"Let me try." Carson took the charging pad from her hand and pressed it against the glass sphere. To his surprise it glowed green and the pad was sucked into the glass, leaving only the wires trailing out. Carson jumped back, fearing losing his fingers.

"What the heck...?" Trix couldn't believe what she saw. The orb pulsed rhythmically and the LEDs on the charger indicated the drone was sucking up electricity.

"I reckon it's, like, Japanese tech," said Eddie. "I think I saw something like this on YouTube..."

He trailed off when the drone began to tremble. At first they thought it was a trick of the light . . . but then the table began to shake and the lights in the room flickered.

Carson took a wary step backwards. "What's happening. . .?"

"I think it might be about to explode," said Eddie, shoving his glasses further up his nose and standing behind Carson for protection.

The sound of a high-pitched whine took Carson straight back to the junk cave. He saw the four propellers start to turn at varying speeds, causing the drone to rock on the desk. The noise rose in pitch, sounding like a squadron of mosquitos. Then they fell silent but continued to turn rapidly. Without a noise, the drone gracefully rose from the table, trailing the power lead behind it.

Trix shouted at the boys. "Stop it!"

Eddie instinctively reached out to grab it, but Carson stopped him. "Watch your fingers!" They both knew the gory dangers of jamming fingers in spinning blades.

The drone shot forward, still trailing the charging cable behind it. It bounced from the wall, switched direction and whooshed at Trix and Carson – forcing them to duck. Then the drone sharply angled towards the ceiling and the light bulb shattered as it flew through it.

Eddie flinched as the drone flew past him so close that it ruffled his hair. There was a bang as the drone bounced off Carson's bookshelf, spilling dozens of novels to the floor.

With a yelp, Eddie found the charging cable had somehow wrapped around his foot – and he tripped over with a thud. The cable yanked free from the drone and whipped across Eddie's backside, causing him to howl in pain.

Carson threw his arms over his head as the drone bounced from wall to wall, floor to ceiling in the darkness. Then, with a final thud, the chaos stopped.

He risked a peek under his arm to see one of the wardrobe doors fall from its hinges. The drone had landed back on the table, the orb brightly glowing in its tail.

"Well ... that was weird," said Eddie, breaking the silence.

"It's looking at us." Even as Carson spoke, the drone's tiny camera flicked between them.

"It's just glitching. I might have overloaded the power," Trix said confidently. "I need to open it up." As she reached for a set of wrenches next to the drone, the camera followed her hand – then the drone hopped backwards on the table with a little VROOM from its propellers. Trix froze. "OK, *that* was weird."

The camera twitched like the head of a nervous insect as it watched them.

"Who's controlling it?" Eddie whispered.

Trix shook her head. "It might be picking up random signals. Wi-Fi, phones, that sort of thing." Although from her tone she didn't believe it, and she still hadn't dared move.

Carson stepped forward. "Can you understand me?" He felt silly talking to a toy.

Eddie whispered into Trix's ear. "That bump on the head must have really—"

Then a girl's soft voice cut through the air. "I can hear you."

There could be no doubt; the drone had spoken to them.

Chapter 7
POWER UP

"Ha-ha, very funny," said Eddie without humour. He pulled a face at Carson. "You're doing this to wind us up, right?" He reached for the drone, but it leapt into the air and hovered out of reach.

Carson took a step forward. "Who is doing that?"

"I am," said the drone as it circled around their heads like an inquisitive fairy. Carson held out his hand and the drone alighted on his palm. "I'm doing this all by myself."

"Are you . . . a robot?"

The drone chuckled teasingly. "Do I look like one? I'm a drone. See?" With that it took off and zipped around the room so fast it became a blur, before coming to a halt and hovering in front of them.

"But you can talk!" Eddie exclaimed. The drone zipped forward and bumped him on the head before retreating. He could feel the propellers buzz dangerously close to his cowlick. "OW!"

"That's for the hammer!"

Trix and Carson laughed as Eddie rubbed his head and mumbled. "Sorry, I didn't..." Then he pulled himself together and pointed at the drone. "I am not arguing with a flying whisk!"

"You are," chirped the drone.

"No, I'm not!"

"And you're losing!" the drone added sassily. It gave a cocky wiggle that further infuriated Eddie.

Carson wiped a tear from his eye as he chuckled. "How can you talk?"

The drone rotated to face him. "You talk to your phones, don't you?"

"And we've got one of those home hubs," said Trix. "It can turn the heat and lights on."

"Sounds rubbish," muttered Eddie. "I don't want to get into an argument with the flipping light switch."

Carson ignored him. "Yeah, but they don't usually have proper conversations back. Not like this."

"They say I'm artificially intelligent."

"Who says?" asked Trix suspiciously.

The light in the drone's tail dimmed, and the little drone spiralled around the table before settling down.

"I'm so tired." It even managed to sound weary. "Could you charge me up again, please? I promise I won't break anything else, but I was in sleep mode and you gave me an unexpected surge."

"Sure," said Carson, switching on the desk lamp and taking a seat so he could study the drone closely. He marvelled at the way the camera was able to swivel around to look at him, a single unblinking eye that somehow managed to look friendly. "Do you have a name?"

Trix paused as she gathered the cables. She looked expectantly at the drone as the light faded even more.

"Huh! It's a drone!" huffed Eddie, who was still rubbing his sore head. "You don't name a bunch of metal and wires."

"My designation is AG-421 Vanta Hawk."

"Then I shall call you Vanta," Carson said with a smile. "I'm Carson. That's Trix, and the grumpy one is Eddie." The drone didn't do anything other than look at each of them in turn.

Trix approached with the charging pad and held it over the dimming sphere. "Are you ready for this?"

"Yes, please. I need a loooonnnng charge."

Trix gingerly attached the pad and, as before, it sank into the orb, leaving only the wires protruding.

"Weird," she muttered under her breath.

Vanta didn't reply. Instead the orb pulsed like a slow heartbeat.

Carson stood up and motioned the others to quietly follow him out of the bedroom, down the hall and downstairs to the kitchen. Pouring beakers of fizzy Coke, they huddled around the table and spoke in low whispers.

"This is amazing!" Carson said before gulping half the drink down.

"Why are we whispering?" whispered Eddie.

"I tell you, according to the web, there is nothing like Vanta out there," said Trix, putting her phone back in her pocket. "She's unique."

"She?" choked Eddie, his Coke fizzing from

his nose. "You don't name your phone." After a thoughtful pause, he added, "Do you?"

"*She* definitely carried me over the scrapyard," Carson said firmly. The more he thought about it, the more he was convinced. But he could tell by the look on Trix's face that she wasn't. "You don't believe me?"

"Talking to us and flying around on her own —"

"*Its* own!" Eddie interjected.

"— is one thing, but flying you out? Really? I think you're getting confused with a movie or something."

Eddie pointed at them both, arms outstretched. "Now that leads me to a good question. Where did she come from?"

Carson couldn't resist raising an eyebrow. "*She?*"

Eddie huffed again. "It! Look, if you wake up dead tomorrow because there is an alien spacecraft in your bedroom, then I'm just going to say 'I told you so.'"

Trix rolled her eyes. "She's not from outer space!"

"What, then? She travelled back in time to stop us saving the world from our robot overlords?" He gave a short triumphant laugh when Trix and Carson exchanged a worried look. "We don't know if she's — it's — safe to be around. What if it's a secret government experiment that went mental and is now trying to destroy the human race? Or maybe a mad scientist could have built her to take over the planet!"

"And then he just dumped her in the scrapyard?" Carson shook his head. "We can ask her tomorrow when she's recharged." Eddie opened his mouth, but before he could utter another wild theory, Carson cut him off. "And I don't care if you think I got hit on the head and imagined everything, Vanta saved me. So I for one don't think she's going to kill us." He looked pointedly at Eddie, then ominously added, "Not all of us, anyway."

Eddie pulled a face but said nothing.

"We shouldn't tell anybody about this," said Trix. The three friends solemnly nodded. "Especially not Kay."

Eddie looked at her blankly.

"Your *sister*!"

Eddie nodded vaguely. "Oh yeah. I just don't call her that. She's too annoying to have a name."

Carson finished his drink, his eyes wandering the ceiling as he thought about the drone above their heads. "I guess we'll get our answers tomorrow."

*

That night, Carson found it difficult to sleep. After half-heartedly tidying his room and reattaching the wardrobe door, he lay on the bed in the dark, lulled by Vanta's steady pulse of light. The drone didn't move or speak again and, just as he heard his father coming home, his eyes closed.

He had a vivid dream of flying, his arms extended wide, the rush of air on his face. It was incredible...

Chapter 8
TEST FLIGHT

Eddie stamped his feet for warmth as a chill breeze blew through the enormous derelict warehouse. It was supposed to be summer, but the weather wasn't cooperating. At least they didn't need to sneak in, as his uncle owned the site and allowed them to use the warehouse to practise racing.

Carson gently took Vanta out of his backpack and placed her on an upturned crate. When he had awoken, the charging cable had been ejected and lay on the desk, but the drone hadn't stirred at all. He was now beginning to wonder if the previous night had actually happened. Just how hard *had* he hit his head?

Eddie kept his distance and examined their broken racing drone. Trix had managed to get two of the engines working, but not enough to make it airborne.

"Terrific," he muttered. "Now we have two drones that don't work."

Their attention was drawn to Vanta when she suddenly lit up with a BEE-BOP that was familiar to Carson. Moments later the engines whirled to life and the drone lifted in the air and flew across to them. The camera angled down to inspect the ruined racing drone.

"Oh dear. What happened here? Did somebody get angry with a hammer?"

Eddie was unnerved by the way the drone's camera stared accusingly at him. "No, he flew it into a wall!" he snapped back, pointing at Carson.

"This was our racing drone," Carson explained. "That's why I was in the scrapyard last night."

Vanta seemed to pause for a moment for speaking. "Ah, yes. Drone racing is becoming a popular sport around the world."

Trix frowned. "You know about it?"

"I just looked it up on the internet."

Eddie was impressed. "Wow. Maybe you can do my homework too?"

"Oh, that'd be *too* easy!" Vanta turned to Carson. "You wanted to find spare parts to replace this?"

Carson nodded. "We were hoping to build one from scratch. They're . . . you're quite expensive."

"Oh, I'm priceless," Vanta chuckled as she pirouetted in the air. "And, since I'm not too busy at the moment, maybe I can be part of your team?"

Carson let out a sigh of relief. While waiting for any signs of life from Vanta, the team had had a whispered discussion about what they should do next with the strange little drone. Carson had felt it was mean to open up Vanta for parts, ignoring Trix, who attempted to remind him that was the original plan.

"And can I remind you it's –" Eddie silently mouthed the word *stolen* as if speaking it aloud would summon the police "– property? We could get arrested!"

"I can race. Watch this!" In a sudden burst of incredible speed, the little drone shot off across the warehouse so fast that she was nothing more than a blur that was lost amongst the warehouse's concrete columns.

Carson spun around, listening for the distinctive buzz of a drone engine, but there was utter silence. Then Vanta suddenly appeared, whooping with delight, as she passed so low overhead that the trio threw themselves flat in the dust.

Vanta stopped dead in the air, then abruptly zigzagged left and right, effortlessly dancing through the barrels, posts and other obstacles they had laid out for training. Then she shot straight up through a broken skylight.

Carson was the first to his feet, slack-jawed with awe.

"Wow. . ."

Vanta plunged straight back down. The move was so savage that Carson threw his hands over his head, expecting the drone to fly straight into him. Instead she hung gracefully in the air, slowly pirouetting nose-down.

Trix couldn't stop herself from clapping. "That was a-ma-zing!"

Carson was breathing hard, as if he had run the circuit himself. "We're going to win everything!"

"That was cool," said Eddie. "Too cool."

The others looked questioningly at him.

"For starters, you're so fast there's no way anyone would believe Carson was flying. That makes us *cheats*. We'd be disqualified, and it's not right."

Carson rolled his eyes. "You and your rules! If we'd listened to you we wouldn't even have a drone right now."

"Duh! You're not listening! We'd be *disqualified*, so we might as well not have a drone at all!"

Trix pulled a Torx from her pocket and waved it at the drone. "But maybe if I could tinker with your power management I could sort that out."

Vanta retreated a little. "Nobody is messing with my undercarriage, young lady."

Trix put the screwdriver away.

Eddie folded his arms defiantly. "There has to be a human pilot. Rules are rules."

Carson guiltily held up a radio controller he had kept in his pocket. "OK. Pair her up to this."

Vanta zipped between the controller and Carson. "*You* want to control *me*, with *that*?"

Eddie looked sidelong at Carson. "I'm afraid

they're the rules, if you want to race with us. Unless you want to go back into the bag?"

Vanta contemplated it for a moment, then quivered in what they interpreted as a nod. "OK then. Let me tune in to your controller." Vanta gave a cute little shimmy, then: "There! Try it."

Carson gently nudged the joystick and Vanta drifted first left, then right. The drone giggled. "That feels so strange!"

"Cool!" Carson applied a little throttle, and Vanta shot forward with a whoop of delight.

"That took me by surprise!" the drone said cheerfully. "Put on your goggles and let's go for a spin."

Trix was laughing as she passed Carson the virtual reality headset. She took her phone out and opened up the racing app so it could receive the drone's signal, then she slid the phone into the helmet to provide the screen. They had long dreamed of getting a proper, high-definition, dedicated headset, but that would have required them to have won a couple of league races at the very least. Carson put the headset's strap tight around his head, wincing as it pressed against his stiches. The phone screen filled his vision as the headset's magnifying lens pulled it into focus. He was now looking at himself, at the video streaming from Vanta's camera.

"Ready when you are!" The drone's perky voice came from the phone's speaker, which was an unusual addition. Their drones had never talked back.

Carson licked his lips, and his thumbs circled the joystick toggles. "Let's see what you're really capable of."

Vanta responded instantly to his controls. Within seconds Carson was flying with the drone – banking around posts, sliding through broken windows into distant extensions of the warehouse. A quick flick of the thumb and the drone jinked vertically upwards, spiralling through an empty skylight and high into the air.

Both Carson and Vanta unleashed screams of delight as they soared high above the industrial estate, the warehouse becoming one of several small blocks below. From this vantage point Carson could see clear across the town, and it struck him that he had never been able to race his drone very far, in case it fell out of range of the controller. Vanta didn't seem to have this problem.

Cackling with exhilaration, he plummeted the drone earthward. He skimmed Vanta low over a lorry pulling into the industrial estate, then turned and buzzed a forklift truck that was loading pallets in an adjacent factory. He saw a couple of angry fists waving at him as they soared over another factory grounds and through a set of concrete pipes that had just been stacked for a delivery.

Then up to the rooftops to effortlessly slalom through smoking chimney pipes – before rolling back through a skylight and into their warehouse. When Carson brought the drone to a dead stop in front of them he was panting hard, as if he'd run the course himself.

He yanked off the goggles and saw the astonished looks on Trix and Eddie's faces. They had witnessed the entire flight on Trix's iPad.

"That was awesome!" Carson said in disbelief. "I mean . . . that was super fast! We are so going to ace this with you!"

Trix fist-bumped Carson, then gave Eddie a lopsided smile. "What do you think?"

"Awesome. I don't see how we can lose!" He didn't share the darker thought at the back of his mind that somebody out there was surely missing this incredible drone. He wondered what they would do to get it back.

Chapter 9
SIGNING UP

The Constructor League race was at the weekend, giving them a couple of days to practise around the warehouse with Vanta. The drone was always in a good mood and eager to fly, but during the night she sat silently on Carson's desk to recharge, while he lay on his bed looking thoughtfully at her.

"How did you end up in the scrapyard?"

For a long moment, Vanta remained silent. Only the occasional flicker of light through her orb gave Carson the impression she was thinking. Eventually she spoke in a weary tone.

"Strong winds . . . blown off course. . ."

Carson waited for more, but it was clear that was all the drone was offering.

"I mean, you're a pretty high-tech … thing. Expensive, I reckon."

"Oh? And how much are you worth?"

A noise from downstairs told Carson somebody was home. A quick glance at the clock told him it was 1:30 in the morning.

"Who lives with you?" Vanta suddenly sounded less exhausted. The glow from her orb brightened inquisitively.

"Just my dad."

He listened to his father's footsteps wearily trudge up the stairs. For a moment they paused outside the door, but Carson didn't expect his dad to check in on him; he never had before. After an uncomfortably long pause, he heard his dad walk away and gently close the door to his own room. Carson let out the breath he hadn't realized he was holding. "So, you were telling me where you came from?"

When he looked back at Vanta, her orb had faded to just a few occasional trickles of light, and the drone didn't say another word for the rest of the night.

*

The trio were out of breath when they dismounted their bikes and craned their necks up at the grubby exterior of the local football stadium.

"I thought this place had been demolished," said Eddie sceptically. "In fact, it's difficult to tell if it hasn't been already."

It had certainly once seen glorious days, but that was probably before they had been born. The only flash of colour amongst the peeling paintwork was a large "Constructor League" banner draped over the entrance. The league's fifty-pound entry fee was everything they had, or rather, what Trix had, topped up with a couple of five-pound notes from the boys.

"I'm only doing this because of our new teammate," she said grudgingly as she paid the fee.

Eddie quickly filled out the registration papers. "They want to know everything. I'm not giving them my address. . ." he muttered.

Carson tapped the team name box. "Carsonators." Eddie grunted, but dutifully filled it in. Then Carson saw the email address Eddie had used. "That's not your email."

Eddie's eyes darted around as he spoke in a whisper. "It's one I use for spam, y'know, when I sign up for free stuff online. It can't be traced to me." Carson shrugged indifferently, causing Eddie to sigh and raise his voice. "We're using a stolen drone! I'm not going to give them our real details! I don't want a criminal record!"

"Sssh! OK, OK," said Carson, indicating Eddie to lower his voice. "Whatever. Let's just get in there."

Eddie handed their entry form back and they walked their bikes into the stadium.

Instantly, everything around them was very different from the grungy car park races they had attended. The outdoor pitch had been converted into an obstacle course, while the sloped seating had flags and markers forming a racetrack that looped around the entire arena. A surprisingly large number of spectators sat at one end of the pitch, watching a large projector screen that would display the action from numerous cameras around the stadium.

"Wow!" said Eddie, wiping the sweat from his brow. "We've hit the big time!"

"It's a bit better than the car park challenge," Carson admitted.

"Let me see," Vanta squeaked from Carson's backpack.

"In a minute," Carson replied quietly as a large man with short, curly brown hair and wearing a garishly bright Hawaiian shirt, blue trainers and khaki cargo shorts, approached them waving an iPad like a fly swatter.

"Hey, kids," he said in a smooth American accent. "This is the team paddock. Spectators sit over there." He pointed to the people sitting at the far end. Then he turned back and was already scrolling through messages on his tablet.

"We are a team," Trix said impatiently.

The man stopped and looked as if he was about to wave them away when Trix raised their entry ticket. His surprise gave way to a doubtful smile.

"OK. Cool. Just a little ... young. And a little sweaty too."

"We had a few technical issues getting here," Eddie said firmly.

"We got lost," Trix clarified.

"What's your team name?"

Carson spoke up before Eddie could. "The Carsonators." He ignored Eddie's groan and elbowed his backpack when he heard an *urgh* from Vanta. The man hadn't seemed to notice.

"Well, Carsonators, everybody is welcome. I'm Marcus Nation. Welcome to my league!" He treated them to a winning smile, as if expecting them to break into applause. Disappointed, he continued, "I put together all these local rounds building to the *championship*." Again he expected a reaction that wasn't forthcoming. He raised an eyebrow. "You know this is the first year the Constructor League's been around, right?"

Carson nodded. "Sure. I read that on the internet."

Nation huffed. "The internet. Terrific. This is gonna be big, you know."

Carson and Trix nodded politely. Eddie gave him a thumbs up.

With a sigh, Nation indicated they should follow him towards the team paddocks. "As you know if you read," he mimicked Carson, "'the internet', we don't have the same rules as the racing leagues. If you can fly it, you can race it." He chuckled. "Although we had one team in Scotland who tried to fly a drone so huge that it couldn't even fit through the first obstacle." He turned, walking backwards as he spoke. "And the course will bite back. I don't want to give anything away, but our spectators are looking for destruction. Big explosions get big cheers."

"Explosions?" Trix swapped a worried glance with Carson.

"Yeah. Should be an interesting race," Nation said as they reached the paddock. It was an unspectacular area filled with workbenches, separated from the rest of the pitch by orange tape strung from poles in the ground.

"We have some mean competition taking part today, so don't let it get you down. It's the taking part that counts."

Carson felt irritated when Marcus winked. The meaning was clear: you don't stand a chance, but thanks for the entry fee.

"Take a bench. See you in the race." He started to walk away, then stopped. "Oh, one more thing. You were late, so you've already missed the sighting lap."

Carson threw up his hands. "Are you serious? We rushed the whole way here!"

The sighting lap allowed racers to test the course out at whatever speed they wanted so they could prepare for the dangers ahead. Without that, Carson would effectively be flying blind.

Marcus Nation winked again and disappeared into the crowd.

They picked their way through the dozen teams who all had their backs to them, their attention on the aircraft on the table. Most drones were in pieces as final adjustments were made. They could see a variety of shapes and tangles of electronics.

They found a free workbench and placed Vanta on it. A quick look around showed the other teams wore furrowed brows, and there was plenty of whispered bickering going on as they feverishly worked on their craft. Trix felt obligated to put her tools on the bench just so it looked as if they had something to do, and Eddie wandered off in search of food.

"Are you sure you're ready for this?" Carson said quietly to Vanta, trying not to move his lips. He didn't want anybody seeing he was talking to his drone.

"Completely," came Vanta's whispered reply.

After several minutes Eddie hurried back, shovelling chips in his mouth. He jabbed Carson in the ribs. "Uh-oh – seen who's over there?" He pointed a greasy finger towards a bench at the far end. The matching T-shirts displaying the AirBlitz logo were enough to freeze Carson's blood and he automatically touched his black eye, remembering.

"I don't think they've seen us," Carson said just as the AirBlitz pilot, a boy called Terry, he recalled, turned around and spotted them. His face turned beetroot red, no mean feat with the acne rash across his cheeks, and he took a step towards them, only to be held back by a teammate's hand on his shoulder. They exchanged a quiet joke without moving their eyes from the Carsonators, which was somehow more intimidating. Then they returned to their drone.

"Well, that's good news," said Eddie brightly. He was famously bad at reading other people's body language. "I don't think they recognized us."

Trix shot a warning glance at Carson, who shook his head. There was little point in getting wound up before the race. There would be plenty of time afterwards.

Daylight quickly faded behind the clouds and the stadium lights dimmed with it, while neon lights brought the course alive with a riot of colour. Animated red and yellow warning chevrons strobed at sharp corners, hoops and tunnels were picked out in Day-Glo blues, while green lights signalled turns, dips and cliffs. A cheer rose through the stadium as dance music blasted from the speakers. Then Marcus Nation appeared on the screen, pumping his fist and encouraging everybody to "make some noise!"

Carson spotted Marcus not far from the team paddocks, at a bank of monitors where a panel of four judges sat, dressed more like rockers than officials. A cameraman slowly paced in front of him, capturing a low angle so that Marcus appeared like a giant on the screen.

"Welcome to the local Constructor League heat!" He smiled as cheers, applause and party horns honked around the stadium. "We have eighteen teams competing today in three head-to-head heats. Each will consist of three laps around the course. In the first heat, the last eight teams will be cut. Then the semi-final will see *only* the winning five racers make it through to the final. Each heat will get progressively tougher and challenge our pilots' wits and skills."

Carson glanced at the teams around them.

There were a few nervous faces, but most of them looked confident and cocky. A few had spotted the Carsonators and laughed as they nudged one another; obviously they thought the kids didn't pose a threat.

Marcus Nation continued. "The winner will receive a thousand pounds. . ."

Eddie started to wiggle his arms and hips in a winning jig, until Trix punched him in the arm to stop.

"Second place wins five hundred, third, fourth and fifth get . . . nothing, zilch, nada! Just the honour of joining the winners in the next stage."

Carson frowned at Eddie. "What next stage?"

Eddie shrugged. "I don't know. I thought this was a one-off."

Marcus continued, ". . .and ultimately at the Constructor League World Championship!"

Now the other teams joined in the cheering and applause.

Trix looked at Carson in surprise. "*World* championship?"

"I didn't really read all the details. . ." In truth, he had only read about the prize money. "Anyway, Eddie's the one who entered us into this."

"Yeah, but I didn't read *everything*. Who reads the small print?"

Marcus Nation's voice boomed through the stadium. "Racers! Take your positions!"

Carson was still reeling from the scale of the competition, and he hesitated as the other teams hurried past to the starting grid. Trix grabbed his hand and pulled him along.

"Now's not the time for stage fright," she growled. With her hair back in its usual spiky formation, she looked like she meant business. "Get your game face on. We can't lose this!"

Eddie scooped Vanta up and followed them to the launch grid where the other competitors had placed their aircraft on small raised platforms. It was the first time they'd properly seen their rivals. The screens around the arena zoomed in on each drone, the team name flashing up underneath.

"Wow. . ." said Eddie as he placed Vanta on the starting line. "A DGI Magic Air! That's a seriously expensive piece of kit!"

"You're so easily impressed," snorted Vanta.

"Sssh!" Carson eyed the other drones. Some were small and could fit into his palm, but most were regular shoebox-sized racing drones, like Vanta but sporting oversized propellers. A couple, including an impressive six-rotored beast – he glanced at the screen to see it was called Sixtus – were the size of microwave ovens.

"This is going to be interesting," said Trix as she put her Bluetooth headset on, while eyeing a large drone that was encased in spikes like a porcupine. Another had a small buzz-saw blade poking from its head, making it resemble a demented beetle.

Carson cleared his dry throat. "This isn't normal racing. . ."

"No." Trix held the VR headset over Carson's head. "Remember he mentioned explosions? I think it's more like a demolition derby." Carson pulled the headset over his eyes and Trix tightened the strap. "You should really have read the website carefully."

"Eddie's the manager. I'm the talent."

"*I'm* the talent," said Vanta over his headset. Trix heard it too and giggled.

Eddie, also listening in, shook his head. "Great, just what our team doesn't need: more big heads."

Marcus Nation's voice boomed over the stadium.

"Don't forget, folks, in the Constructor League, anything goes! This is a full-contact sport!"

"What does 'full contact' mean?" came Vanta's voice over his headset.

"Um..." Looking from Vanta's point of view, he could see the camera was twitching side to side to get a peek at the other crafts. "Vanta, please stop doing that, it's making me feel dizzy. Just look straight ahead."

"Racers! Power those engines!" yelled Marcus Nation.

Across the start line, sixteen electric engines buzzed to life. Some had been kitted out to sound deeper and more menacing. Carson gently nudged the throttle controller and Vanta's engines silently spooled up.

Vanta sounded concerned. "Are you sure you don't want me to steer?"

"I've got this," Carson assured her.

"Get ready!"

Animated numbers on the giant video display started the countdown. Five ... then the audience chimed in.

"Four!"

"Three!"

"Two!"

Carson's mouth felt dry and his palms became sweaty. He inhaled a deep breath.

"One!"

Chapter 10
THE FIRST RACE

Almost every other drone was in the air before Carson pushed the throttle forward.

"Let's go!" screamed Vanta in his headset.

Carson shoved the throttle to max with one thumb, the other tilting Vanta forward. The little drone was near the back of the pack due to their late entry, the other drones appearing ahead as a jumble of blinking lights.

The crowd cheered as the aircraft entered their first long lap around the stadium. They were moving so fast that they appeared as streaks of light. The motion-tracking cameras dotted around the course were able to pick the leading drones so the crowd could see clearly.

Marcus Nation provided commentary. "It's no surprise to see Logan46 in the lead, followed by AirBlitz and the Tornados. . ."

"Logan46?" groaned Carson. He hadn't seen them in the paddock, and he had hoped that they'd have been satisfied taking home the prize from the other racing league. Did they have to win *everything*? "Eddie, why didn't you warn me they were here too? That's your job!"

Eddie's muffled reply came from behind him and indicated his mouth was crammed with chips. "They didn't give me the team roster because we were late. I can't do everything."

"You haven't done *anything*," came Trix's voice from his right. She always stood there during a race, watching the video feed on her iPad. She was not only the team's mechanic, but essentially a co-pilot. She kept an eye on the track ahead to warn Carson of potential problems and her software usually allowed her to monitor their drone's vital statistics – engine RPM, temperature, battery life – but Vanta was revealing no data. "Don't worry about them. Just worry about not coming last."

That was easier said than done. Without a sighting lap, Carson didn't know what lay ahead or how Vanta would cope with them. He thought it best to keep back and see how the other competitors coped.

A drone in front of him was suddenly struck from the side by the craft with spikes. The thin spars tore into the smaller drone's propellers, shattering them. The broken drone spun off uncontrollably into the darkness.

"Now I know what 'full contact' means," said Vanta apprehensively.

"Wipeout! That was nasty!" Marcus Nation yelled cheerfully. "Destructor took out RogueBladez with zero mercy!"

Carson banked behind Destructor, thinking at least he wouldn't be a threat, as long as he didn't dare overtake. The outer part of the track completed, the drones followed the green arrows into the obstacle section. It was the usual variety of tunnels, hoops and blocks of concrete positioned to form up-and-under barriers. Carson easily sped through them. Three other drones were not so lucky.

One smashed straight into a concrete block at full speed and actually exploded in a shower of sparks – much to the crowd's delight.

Vanta wasn't enjoying herself. "This is barbaric! Are we back in ancient Rome?"

Carson was too focused on piloting her through a tunnel. Only when they were out of the obstacle course and back on the track for lap two did he recall his history lessons.

"That makes us a gladiator! That's pretty cool."

"Huh. A pretty slow gladiator," Vanta muttered.

"She has a point," said Trix. "Can't you speed up? At least we're not last. There's somebody else behind us." There was the briefest of pauses. "Oh wait. They're down and out with an engine problem. Yup, we're last."

To add insult to injury, Marcus Nation spoke out. "The battle for first place remains between Logan46 and AirBlitz. And look, who woulda thunk it? Amazingly, bringing up the pack in last place are our kid competitors, the Carsonators."

"I'm going to short-circuit from shame," growled Vanta. "I thought you said you could fly?"

"I can't believe even my drone's giving me grief!"

Carson pushed the throttle forward. "Right. Let's see what you've got!"

Overtaking Destructor on a bend was effortless. The lumbering drone tried to bank into Vanta, but Carson easily avoided the spikes. On the straight he effortlessly weaved through the next six competitors.

"See ya! Wouldn't wanna be ya!" sang Vanta as they passed by, then turned on to the obstacle course.

Carson had been anticipating the same easy obstacles, but on this lap the race organizers had spiced things up. A thin layer of smoke hung in the air, forcing the racers to slow down so abruptly that one was savagely rear-ended, bumping the drone into a concrete post hidden in the smoke. It broke apart on impact.

Carson pushed Vanta onward. The up-and-under concrete slabs were next – except this time they were moving, powered by a series of motorized wheels that turned the gaps into vengeful mouths that chomped at the drones.

"Carson!" Vanta said in alarm.

"I see it. Don't worry." Carson pulled his drone

into a hover, alongside several other competitors, and he watched the pattern of clashing slabs repeat itself. "I've got this," he muttered, more to assure himself than the drone.

"Vanta, can you take over if you need to?" Eddie asked over their headsets. He had been watching every moment on the giant screen.

"I'm not sure. And if I could, definitely not quick enough to avoid a crash. . ."

"OK, Carson, no pressure. Try not to trash another drone."

A small racer next to Vanta suddenly bolted forward when the pilot saw a gap opening up between the slabs. But he had miscalculated, and a third slab behind smashed down, crushing the drone as flat as a pancake.

Carson heard Vanta gasp but didn't have time to hesitate. He sent all the power to the engines and bolted forward. Several of his competitors did the same, including Logan46. Carson now found himself amongst the leading pack as they weaved through the traps and shot into the tunnel.

Sweat had built up under Carson's visor. One bead managed to make it to his eye, making it sting.

He blinked furiously, accidentally wobbling Vanta side to side.

"You hit someone!" Trix suddenly yelled.

"Carson! Stop that!" Vanta snapped in his ear.

Carson regained his sight just as they shot out of the tunnel and swept up on to the racetrack for a final lap. A quick check revealed he had clashed rotors with a smaller drone, knocking it to the back of the pack.

"I'm fine, thanks for asking," Vanta said with a trace of irritation.

Carson positioned himself behind AirBlitz, who was hanging in third place. "Sorry. But we've got this. A straight lap around the track and we're in the lead."

He was vaguely aware of Marcus Nation's commentary, which he had managed to drown out to almost a background buzz. "Logan46 takes the lead, Sixtus is next, followed by AirBlitz! They have everything to race for."

"We've got company," Vanta warned him. Her camera briefly glanced to the side, revealing the buzz-saw drone edging closer. The spinning blade extended out towards Vanta. She quickly looked away.

"I can't see—" said Carson.

There was a sudden white flash and Carson saw the flaming remains of the buzz-saw drone cut across his path.

"What just happened?"

"There's something on the track ahead!" said Trix urgently. "Something big! Go left!"

Carson didn't hesitate. His thumbs moved the stick before he saw that a lorry trailer had been deliberately parked across the track, forcing the racers back on to the obstacle course earlier than before. Logan46 and AirBlitz made last-minute turns – both drones raising sparks from their undercarriages as they scraped along the trailer.

A more cumbersome drone made the turn too late. Three propellers on one side sheared off, sending it into an unrecoverable spin that took out a competitor behind. Carson couldn't help but cackle with dark delight as he edged into the lead.

The detour meant that they had been shunted on to the obstacle course from the wrong side. The last two laps had given the racers a false sense of security, but now going through it backwards was completely unfamiliar and involved a series of blazing hoops that hadn't been there earlier.

"Hot! Hot! Hot!" squeaked Vanta as they flew through the flames.

"Sorry!"

"The other two are right on my tail!" she warned.

Carson marvelled as a small video appeared in the corner of his visor, showing his rivals just behind him. He hadn't even noticed Vanta had a camera there.

"I'm going flat-out!" Carson shouted, carried away by the excitement.

"I can go much faster, but your radio receiver is holding me back. If you give me control..."

"I've got it."

"But Carson—"

"I'm in control!"

"They're gaining on me!"

Sure enough, Carson watched as the two drones drew either side of him. They were bigger and their intentions were clear – to swat Vanta between them. All three entered the tunnel at the same time. Carson could see them both move slightly apart as Vanta's camera panned quickly between them in panic. Then they swooped sideways for the crush!

Carson pulled the throttle back hard. Vanta

slowed almost instantly and he laughed out loud as the two bullies collided with one another as they raced ahead. Unfortunately they hadn't caused any serious damage to one another, and now Carson was relegated to third place.

Fourth – as Sixtus swept past him. Vanta and Trix were already screaming "Go! Go! Go!" at him as he accelerated forward. But try as he might, AirBlitz and Logan46 were now too far ahead. Vanta banked on the final straight, the animated neon arrows now pointing towards the finish line. The race was on for third place. He didn't hear a peep from Vanta as he drew alongside Sixtus. The bigger drone attempted to bump him, but a quick jiggle of the stick put Vanta just out of reach. The move had cost Sixtus precious speed, and Carson inched ahead and before he knew it—

"The race is over!" screamed Marcus Nation. "AirBlitz take gold, Logan46 silver and – from the back of the pack, the surprising newcomers – the Carsonators steal third place!"

Chapter 11

EVERY LOSER WINS

Carson sighed as he watched the AirBlitz and Logan46 teams standing on the podium, accepting their prizes before the applauding audience. Unlike most other sports, there was no bronze medal.

"Third place is for losers in this game," said Carson angrily. "We should have easily won this."

They examined Vanta, who now sat on the workbench not looking any worse for wear.

"If you'd let me take over," said Vanta, who seemed just as angry as Eddie. "I could've out-raced them all."

Trix was examining the radio control unit. "I

think the frequency from this is interfering with your power performance." She regarded the controller thoughtfully. "Maybe if I can switch frequency that will help?"

Vanta used her fans to reposition herself on the table to look at Carson. "If you'd let me do all the flying, we would have won!"

"We may be many things, but we're not cheats," said Eddie. "It has to be human controlled. And that I *did* read on the website," he added defensively.

"It might be cheating," sighed Carson as he watched the winners on the big screen as they performed a victory dance, "but it's as bad as losing to those morons."

"Excuse me?" The voice behind made them all start. Carson turned to see a girl with freckles and a red ponytail poking through the back of a baseball cap. She looked a year older than Carson. A VR visor hung from her neck, and she was holding a remote control that had more switches and dials than he had ever seen. "Carsonators, right?"

Carson nodded mutely.

"Were you ... just talking to your drone?" She stood on tiptoes to look over his shoulder.

Carson immediately moved to block her view. His cheeks burned cherry red and he felt his tongue flop around his mouth uselessly.

Eddie nodded. "Yes, he was. He banged his head and lost a few IQ points. He's down to single figures now."

Carson glared at him to shut up. "It's just our team debrief."

For a moment the girl regarded the Carsonators with suspicion, but then shrugged and smiled. "I'm India. Just wanted to say that was some gnarly flying out there."

"Oh, thanks." Carson felt his cheeks burn. "You know, if it wasn't for that rubbish Sixtus –" he laughed nervously and nudged Trix, who stared unsmiling at the girl "– I mean, six rotors? Give me a break. Somebody needs help!"

The girl's smile turned to ice. "That's my drone."

Carson suddenly felt sick inside. "Yeah, that's what I mean. It's great..."

Any friendliness in the girl's voice vanished. "Well, I just wanted to say good luck next time. You'll need it." She turned abruptly away and disappeared amongst the crowd.

Trix's voice dripped with sarcasm. "You handled that so well."

"Heartbeat elevated, facial temperature rising. Looks like you fancy somebody," sang Vanta before joining Trix and Eddie in laughing.

"No, I don't!" muttered Carson as he felt his cheeks burn.

"Look on the bright side," said Eddie. "We may have lost the race, and have no money left... Oh, wait, there isn't a bright side."

Carson wasn't in the mood to argue. He carefully slid Vanta into the backpack as Marcus Nation nudged his way through the crowd to find them.

"Hey, guys!" he panted, fighting for breath. "I was hoping I'd catch you before you dashed. That was some impressive racing out there!" He nudged Carson in the arm. "I mean, seriously awesome stuff. We had you pegged to lose! I even lost money betting against you."

Carson could hear Vanta say something from the confines of the backpack, but he gave it a shake to silence her. Nation hadn't appeared to notice.

"Any-hooo, third place means you're through to the next heat."

Carson, Trix and Eddie had completely forgotten. They looked at one another in surprise.

"There really is a bright side?" gasped Eddie.

"Sure is. The first five all go to the next stage, so you're in! It's next week in London. Twenty-five teams battling it out to represent the UK."

"Represent the whole country?"

"That's right. The Constructor League's first UK finals! And then it only gets bigger! We'll email you the details. Just wanted to say, well done."

With that Marcus Nation was lost in the crowd as he congratulated the other runners-up.

Trix and Eddie were talking, but Carson didn't hear a word. He couldn't believe that things were finally going right.

The trio left the stadium, excitedly talking over one another. Eddie even burst into a verse of "We Are the (Almost) Champions..."

None of them were aware of a pair of suited figures watching them intently from the judges' panel. Nor did they notice how the figures appeared to talk into their wrists, almost as if they had microphones hidden away there...

Chapter 12

THINGS THAT GO BUMP...

Carson stopped outside his house and remained on his bike, eyeing the dark windows. The terraced street was very quiet and lit with yellow street lights that did little to dispel the darkness. His father's car wasn't in the driveway, so he had no reason to sneak inside, but the thought of walking into the empty house at night always filled him with sadness.

He wheeled his bike into the side passage and locked the gate. Then he pulled his key out and slid it into the front door . . . once again pausing.

"Are you OK?" came Vanta's muffled voice from his backpack. "I'm detecting elevated signs of stress."

"I'm OK," Carson lied, and turned the key, nudging the squeaking door open with his toe. Inside, he immediately put the hall light on before shutting the door. Then he removed Vanta from his pack and placed her on a small table filled with unopened mail.

"Doesn't your mother live with you?" Vanta asked innocently. She couldn't see Carson's face, but saw his shoulders tense.

"Your batteries must be drained," he said evasively. "I need to plug you in."

Vanta remained silent as he made a sandwich from the leftovers in the fridge, then picked her up and headed to his room. He hooked up the charging pack and the little drone sat silently on his desk, her orb pulsing steadily.

"What happens if you completely run out of power?"

"What happens if you stop breathing?" she replied.

The answer upset Carson more than he liked to admit. He took to his iPad to read more about the Constructor League they had just taken part in. Founder Marcus Nation, he learned, had made his fortune from fidget spinners. Nation had always loved drone racing and decided to create his own action-packed league. Media companies had even bid for the rights to show the UK final on TV.

"Your father works several jobs, doesn't he?"

Carson was surprised that Vanta was active. "Uh, yes. He's always working. I think he prefers it to spending time here. . ." He stopped himself from saying *with me* out loud.

"And you didn't answer the question about your mother."

The text on Carson's iPad had become a blur. He was lost in a long silence, unable to form the words to answer Vanta's question.

Aware he hadn't spoken for a long time, he looked sidelong at Vanta. The drone hadn't moved and showed no further signs of activity. He closed the browser and checked his messages. There were dozens of them from Trix and Eddie, eagerly relaying the race to their network of online friends. There must have been about fifteen people throwing congratulations and asking questions. He considered joining the conversation, but he hadn't met any of them, nor had he joined in the group chats online.

If anything, it made him feel quite lonely, as if he was watching a party from the doorway and never taking part. He turned the tablet off and laid it on his bedside table.

"You never told me what happened to that buzz-saw drone."

Vanta gave a little flutter on her forward fans, repositioning herself to look directly at Carson. "I think it developed engine trouble."

"That was quite convenient." He didn't believe Vanta's answer, and the memory of Eddie's warning that she may be dangerous briefly swam back to mind, before he dismissed the thought.

"Yes. We were lucky."

Carson turned off the bedside lamp and pulled the duvet over him. He instantly felt a wave of tiredness creep through his body. The fast-moving events of the day had finally caught up with him.

"You're one of a kind," said Carson with a yawn.

"I am that." The reply came with a warm hint of pride.

"So where did you come from? And why would anybody throw you away?"

"Questions, questions, questions..."

"And no answers, answers, answers." Carson wanted to feel annoyed, but the truth was he enjoyed having somebody to talk to at night.

"You worry too much, Carson Lox."

Carson drifted into a warm dream ... but somewhere at the back of his mind he wondered how Vanta knew his full name. He didn't recall telling her. . .

The wind on his face felt cool and refreshing. Carson spread his arms wide, enjoying the sensation of flying through the wide canyon ... no, the *Grand* Canyon. That was it. The vivid orangey-brown walls towered above him, turning red in the dying rays of the sun. The wind increased ... then seemed to snap at his ears as something brushed past them.

"Wake up!"

Carson jolted awake with a start. It was still dark. His hand went to swat whatever was buzzing around his ear. The light from Vanta bobbed before his eyes, and he realized the breeze from his dream was caused by the downwash of her propellers buzzing too close to his face.

"What are you doing?" he said with alarm.

"Ssssh!" Vanta cut him off in a low voice. "I heard a noise downstairs."

Carson groaned and closed his eyes. "That'd be Dad coming home."

Vanta zipped across to his door and whispered, "It's not your father."

Carson bolted upright in bed. He'd heard a noise too: a soft shuffling made by somebody trying not to make a sound. His dad wouldn't care how much noise he made and the lights would have all been on in the hallway. Instead, the gap under Carson's door remained dark.

It must be a burglar! His first instinct was to call the police. He groped for his phone on the bedside table. It wasn't there.

He felt a pang of panic. Where had he left it? With horrible clarity he suddenly recalled placing it on the kitchen table as he made his sandwich.

Vanta drifted silently to the door. "Let's check it out!"

"No! I need to call the cops."

Which meant creeping into the kitchen. He fumbled under his bed and found a battered cricket bat. At least having the heavy wood in his hand made him feel braver. He gingerly climbed from bed and tiptoed across his room. Taking a deep breath, he slowly opened his door. He'd had enough practice to do so without making the hinges groan.

"Entering stealth mode!" whispered Vanta, her tail light extinguishing. In the darkness, Carson couldn't even hear her spinning rotors.

Beyond, the landing was dark and quiet and there was no sign of Vanta. Before he could open his mouth to call to her, there was more scuffling from downstairs, followed by muted whispering. There were two intruders and, judging from their tone, one was a woman.

Carson's blood turned to ice when he heard a gentle creak from the bottom step. Somebody was climbing the stairs!

He considered dashing back to his bedroom and hiding, but that would only be cornering himself. He pressed himself against the wall just to the side of the staircase and raised the cricket bat. He held his breath and the hammering of his heart almost drowned out the approaching footsteps.

The air shifted next to him, signalling the arrival of the intruder.

With a battle cry that startled even him, Carson stepped out, the bat held before him. It was too dark to make out any features, but it was obviously a man standing in front of him, yelping in surprise. Carson spotted something gun-like with flashing lights in his hand. Presuming it was a weapon, he swung the bat, putting all his weight into it. There was an explosion of air as the bat slammed home into the man's chest. Carson had been expecting him to fall back the way he came, but the intruder groaned and doubled over in agony.

Before Carson could swing again there was a rush of movement as Vanta darted past him on a collision course for the man's head. Carson watched in astonishment as the man was pitched backwards, sailing over the second intruder, who stood several steps behind.

The man landed hard in the hallway below and tumbled out of the still-open front door. There was just enough illumination coming through the door from the street light outside, to see the outline of a woman. She had turned around to follow the path of her colleague. Carson caught blonde hair poking from under a black cap. She started to turn back to face him, raising a strange boxy pistol at him – just as Vanta dropped down in front of her and spun around so that the orb from her tail faced her. The drone emitted a sharp blinding strobe light. Carson looked away, covering his eyes with his forearm.

There was a shrill scream, followed by the sound of a quick retreat. Then the door slammed shut.

Carson was shaking when he sat at the top of the stairs. He could still see the afterimage of the bright flash; fortunately, it was slowly fading. Vanta hovered close to him.

"Don't worry, they've gone. They won't come back."

"How do you know?"

"Trust me. Your heart rate is elevated. Take a few deep breaths." Carson did so. With each long breath he felt better. "Go and make yourself a hot chocolate. You'll feel better. I'd make you one myself, but I don't have hands." She wiggled two of her propellers, making Carson smile, despite his trembling.

"Who were they?"

"Just some common thieves. Maybe they saw you at the race and were just chancing their luck. Don't let it worry you."

Carson remained on edge for the rest of the night and only turned his bedside light off when he heard the more familiar thumps of his dad arriving home. All the hall lights came on as he wearily ascended the stairs and, as usual, paused outside Carson's door.

Normally his father would walk away after a few moments, but this time he stayed. Something was wrong. Then he heard the door handle squeal as it was turned, but his dad still didn't enter.

With a gulp, Carson realized he had left Vanta in full view on the table and he knew his dad's view on drone racing. He sat up, ready to throw the discarded jacket at the end of his bed over Vanta.

Too late. The door opened and his dad stepped inside.

"Hey, pal, are you awake?" Caught sitting upright, Carson couldn't pretend otherwise. His father was immediately drawn to the glow from Vanta. "What's this? You haven't been wasting your money on those silly toys again, have you?"

"It's not. . ." Carson stopped himself. There was no use arguing. "I was given it. It's broken, though. Doesn't work."

"Good. You should be doing something ... constructive." He searched for an example as he looked around the posters on Carson's wall. "A sport or something."

"Drone racing is a sport."

His dad gave him a look that brimmed with impatience. Then he sighed, his voice softening. "You forgot to lock the front door again. You need to be careful, someone could just walk right in."

"Sorry."

His dad awkwardly rubbed his hands together, searched for something else to say, and duly failed. He headed for the door. "Night, then."

As his dad left, Carson lay back down. Regardless of whether the front door was locked, he was certain he wouldn't sleep for the rest of the week.

Chapter 13
THE WATCHERS

The next few days rolled along as summer holidays do, with long, hazy days that bled into humid nights. For the most part they practised racing Vanta around the warehouse. Trix had her nose in a set of online instructions while her hands tinkered with the electronic guts of the radio controller.

"You're giving out a lot of weird frequencies," she said to Vanta. "They're definitely interfering with the controller, which is slowing you down, and I don't think there is anything I can do about it. Can you turn something off?"

"Not really. I don't quite know what signals I'm sending out. I can't help it."

"Like BO," Eddie chimed in as he read the long list of terms and conditions on the Constructor League website.

Trix and Carson frowned.

"Well, you can't control your BO and people still complain." He turned back to Carson's iPad and continued reading the league's racing rules, unaware of his friends' confused frowns.

It seemed an age had passed since the burglars had broken into Carson's house. He had told the others, who had all heard of several similar break-ins that night.

"My mum's calling it a crime wave," Eddie added with some relish.

As Vanta had predicted, the intruders hadn't come back, but Carson was still worried. He couldn't find any evidence that the front door had been tampered with, which meant either he had left it unlocked – he was certain he hadn't – or they had been more than just common thieves.

"If you're worried, I'll take her," said Trix.

Carson eyed the screwdriver in her hand and

caught Vanta's camera nervously flicking between that and him.

"It's fine," he assured her. "After the beating we gave them, I'm sure they won't be back."

"It's not as if you have much worth stealing anyway," Eddie pointed out.

Carson was hard pressed to disagree. Like most of the stuff in the house, the TV was older than him, and they had no valuables to speak of.

Eddie stopped reading the iPad and rubbed his eyes. "You know we still can't afford to get to London next weekend."

The emailed invitation for the semi-finals had arrived and, duty-bound as manager, he had spent an entire evening reading all the small print and replying to every query. The event was to be held in a huge converted warehouse in the East End docks. It would even be televised on a sports channel. It would bring together the top five qualifiers from the five heats held across the country and came with a whopping ten-thousand-pound prize. Plus, the winner would go through to the world championship.

It was too good to be true.

Eddie ticked off each point on his fingers: "We

can't afford to get there. We can't afford to *stay* there, and we can't afford to come home." Then he looked slyly at Trix. "Unless. . ."

Trix didn't even bother looking up. "Forget it, *Edward*. We spent the last of my birthday loot in the last race, and look what I have to show for that."

"But your parents are loaded!"

Trix threw him an irritated look. "They're not *loaded*, and they won't give me money for this. I've already asked! So just shut up about it."

Although her house was three times bigger than his own, Carson decided not to join in the argument. "What about you, Eddie?"

"You know how weird my parents are. They freak out when I go into town. They won't let me go all the way to London. I tried explaining about the competition."

"What did they say?"

"Perhaps when you're eighteen," he said, mimicking his mother's voice as he took his glasses off to clean on the hem of his grubby shirt.

"Then we can't go." Carson kicked a stone but felt little satisfaction as it bounced across the floor and struck an old oil drum with a deep clang. "There'll be other competitions to enter," he said wistfully. "You never know, we might even win enough to pay Trix back for all the entry fees and drone parts she's shelled out for in the past. What do you think, Vanta?"

Over the last few days they had started talking to her like a proper member of the team. Even Eddie seemed more at ease around her.

"I enjoyed the race, despite you holding me back." Perched above on a beam, she silently spun her rotors. "It's good to be back in the air after ... the scrapyard."

The three friends exchanged glances. Vanta had deliberately not answered any questions about her past and, just for a moment, it sounded as if she was about to reveal something. But after an awkward pause, it was clear the drone would say no more.

Carson looked at his watch. It was getting late in the afternoon, and they had agreed with Eddie's uncle not to hang around the warehouse after the other surrounding businesses had closed for the day. "Want to go for a last spin?"

Vanta didn't respond. It was as if she had frozen to the beam.

"Hey, Vanta! What's wrong?" Trix tapped the controller in her hand, wondering if she had somehow paralyzed the little machine. "Vanta?"

Eddie picked up a stone, ready to chuck it at her. "Maybe her batteries are flat?"

"Throw that stone if you dare," muttered Vanta without moving. "There's somebody outside."

There was something in her tone that made the hairs on Carson's arm rise. He'd been on edge ever since the break-in. Without a word he crossed to a large window. Patches of dirty glass still clung to the wire mesh across it. Carson ducked behind the sill and peered out. A black van was moving slowly down the road, weaving between discarded blocks of concrete and the tufts of head-high wild weeds growing amongst the cracks. Eddie and Trix joined him.

"Tinted windows!" whispered Eddie. "Nice!"

"They could be just lost," Trix said hopefully.

Eddie shook his head. "No. They're definitely looking for something."

"Us," said Carson firmly. "Ever since the race."

Trix edged away from the window. "There were a lot of other racers there who didn't look too happy with us."

"And you insulted that girl you fancied," Eddie added, nudging Carson in the side.

Carson blushed. "Shut up, I don't fancy her. And I don't think she'd track us down just to try and intimidate us."

"I think *somebody* wants to." Trix moved back from the window as the van drew closer, moving no faster than walking pace. "I mean, Terry from AirBlitz hates us. They all know we're supposed to be going to London. I wouldn't put it past them to try and sabotage us."

Carson recalled the people who had entered his house. Could that have been Terry and his mates? As unlikely as it seemed, he wouldn't put it past the AirBlitz team to resort to dirty tricks to win. Especially now the prize money was so high.

Vanta buzzed over their heads to peer out. "We should leave via the back way so they don't see us."

Nobody argued with that. They quickly climbed through the broken shutters at the back of the warehouse and across a neighbouring field before they were finally on the road back into town. Only at that point did Carson open his pack for Vanta to swoop inside.

The friends agreed that, unless a miracle happened and they could suddenly afford to enter the UK finals, they should perhaps stop racing for the rest of the week.

Just to play it safe.

With his friends busy with family commitments that evening, Carson wasn't feeling terribly happy about being stuck home with his father, on his one regular evening off. However, he felt even worse when he discovered his dad was quickly tying his bootlaces in the kitchen.

"I'm covering somebody who called in sick, so I'm going to be home late." He nodded at Carson's backpack containing the drone. "What've you been doing?"

Carson's grip on his pack's strap tightened. "Nothing. Just hanging with the others..."

His dad looked unconvinced, but he nodded. "I was thinking about this weekend. Maybe I could juggle my shifts around. We could eat out? Go bowling? You like bowling."

"I hate bowling, remember? I'm rubbish at it." Carson immediately regretted the words and quickly turned away – only to see a large bouquet of flowers on the table.

"They're for Mum. You remember what day it is?"

Carson had completely forgotten, yet he still nodded. The thought of being home alone became a sickly hollow feeling in his chest. He felt tears well, but refused to let his dad see them. Out the corner of his eye, he could see his dad was about to put a hand on his shoulder ... but stopped himself.

"I'll be late. Remember to lock up."

With a quick glance at his watch, he left. Carson wiped the tears away and ran his snotty nose across his sleeve. Only when he heard the front door close and the car start up did he hurry to lock up and check the windows were fastened firmly. His appetite had vanished so, clutching his cricket bat, he went to his room and sat on his bed with the lights low, peering into the street for strangers.

"This is not normal behaviour," Vanta noted as she buzzed around the room. Since they had arrived back, the little drone kept flitting restlessly from table to floor to the top of the wardrobe.

"If anybody tries to break in again, I'll be ready."

"Don't worry about that. I'm here. I'll watch over you." There was a long silence. "Are you crying?"

"No," sniffed Carson, wiping a tear from his cheek.

Vanta hovered in front of him. "Yes, you are."

Carson wiped his eyes and tried to turn away. Vanta zipped in front of him no matter which way he turned.

"I'm sorry," she said softly. "I'm not very good at this type of thing. In fact, I've never done it before."

"What sort of thing?"

"Feelings sort of things. The people I used to talk to weren't as . . . *nice* as you. I calculate this is about your mother, since she isn't here, and from what your father was saying I can postulate that—"

Carson sniffed. "She died. She was ill and she died last year . . . last year today."

"Oh." After a quick flutter left and right, as if she didn't know what to do with herself, Vanta added, "How did that happen?"

Carson shrugged. "She fell ill. Didn't get better. What does it matter? There's thousands of bad things that can happen . . . and they do. She died."

He had, of course, cried a lot at the time, and

not a day went by when he didn't feel her absence. And every night he missed hearing her read a story to him. That had been a while ago, but still those nights were his fondest memory. And he had never felt the need the share it with anybody, especially his friends.

"I used to like it when she read to me, to help me sleep. The stories would make me dream of bigger and better things. Like travelling, or being able to fly!"

"I help you fly."

Carson smiled. "Yes, you do." Then he laughed. "My dad would go mental if he knew. When Mum fell ill he became so . . . mean. Tough. Kept telling me to grow up." A sad smile crossed his face. "But my mum . . . she would have driven us to London." He yawned and lay down on his bed, propping the bat on the side so it was just within reach. He closed his eyes. "Making it to that race, she would have been so proud."

"What was your favourite story that she used to read to you? Mine is 'The Gingerbread Man'."

"How do you know that story?" The words barely escaped his mouth as he yawned again.

"I just read several thousand of them on the internet."

"You're a quick reader. Why that one?"

"I can relate to it. Listen: *'Run, run as fast as you can. You can't catch me, I'm the Gingerbread Man...'*" Vanta giggled. "That's like me. Would you like me to read you a story?"

"I used to love my mum reading *Around the World in Eighty Days.*"

"Ah, Jules Verne," Vanta said knowingly. *"Mr Phileas Fogg lived, in 1872, at No. 7, Saville Row, Burlington Gardens..."* she began softly.

If somebody was listening outside the door, they would have heard the slow, heavy breathing of a boy as he slid into the arms of deep sleep...

Chapter 14
A WELCOME GIFT

"I don't believe it." Carson reread the email for the dozenth time.

"It's a confirmation for train tickets and a hotel booking for our team," Eddie said. "Came through this morning with a note attached saying 'good luck!' I thought it was from you." He glanced at Trix.

"Why would I do that?" Trix held up her hands, baffled. "You've both managed to spend all my money several times over."

Carson snapped his fingers. "Marcus Nation! You remember he made a point in coming over to talk to us. He was impressed."

Trix looked doubtful. "Why would *he* do that?"

"Because we're so young – maybe that helps him get more attention?"

"Who cares! We're going!" Eddie held up his hand to high-five her. Trix didn't move, other than to shake her head.

"In that case, we only have a couple of days to solve this controller problem, if Carson's going to push Vanta to the max." She bent down to look at Vanta. "You up for that?"

"I'm in it to win it!" whooped Vanta, performing a little barrel roll.

While Trix tinkered with the controller, Carson worried about how they would manage to avoid their parents for a whole weekend. His dad would be easy enough to fool, but for the other two it was a problem.

"I could say I'm having a sleepover party at mine?" he suggested.

Eddie shook his head. "Two problems." He counted on his fingers. "One, Trix's parents will want to know who else is staying. Two, my parents never let me sleep over. They don't let me go far. They don't let me do *anything*. Three. My sister is a monster. She'll find out, she always does somehow, and then she'll rat on me and my summer will be over. And probably next summer too!"

That gave Carson an idea. "But Kay's eighteen, isn't she? That makes her an adult."

"Technically..."

"Then we need her on our side."

Eddie shook his head so ferociously that he felt dizzy and almost fell over. "Uh-uh. No way. Absolutely not. Impossible! We are not telling her *anything*."

"Sure. Totes. Whatever." Kay looked up briefly from her phone to check the three of them were still there.

Eddie was dumbfounded. "You'll actually do this for us?"

"That's what I said, Edwardo."

Eddie flinched. He hated *Edwardo* more than his actual name, and especially the way she spoke it in a momentous drawl that she thought sounded cool.

"I said yes, didn't I? Now let's get our business straight. You win this little competition and you'll give me *half* the prize money just for covering for you three little shrimps?"

Carson nodded solemnly. "That's right. Three hundred pounds straight to you if we win."

"And if you lose...?"

Edward laughed. He had meant it to sound casual, but it came out as a stressed squeak. "Even losing we get fifty quid. And you can have all of that."

"That sounds kinda weird."

Trix shrugged. "Well, that's drone racing. It's just a weird little sport."

That seemed to satisfy Kay. She nodded and, with a flick of her fingers, motioned they could go. Eager not to be around her for any longer than necessary, Eddie grabbed his friends by the elbow and led them out.

"Boy, your sister is thick," Trix whispered.

"Hey, Edwardo," Kay called after them. "In case you think of, like, trying to rip me off..." She held up her phone and played back a video taken minutes earlier.

"I need you to lie to Mum and Dad," said the recording of Eddie. Kay stopped the video. "Close the door as you go," she said.

"Maybe not so thick," said Carson quietly, once they were out in the hallway again.

"What if we lose?" Eddie was already stressing, barely able to talk in a whisper. "I can't afford fifty quid!"

Trix patted him on the shoulder. "Then it looks like your summer will be over. You better just hope we win."

Still wary of running into any potential saboteurs, they decided not to practise at the warehouse. Instead, Eddie had scouted a place in the woods, and they sent Vanta soaring through the trees at speed.

It proved to be a fresh challenge for Carson, as the gusting breeze and an unexpected light shower affected his control on Vanta. Throughout it all the little drone couldn't help but giggle as she ducked under tree limbs and sailed over fallen logs; spun around mighty oak trunks and between the most crooked of branches. She seemed to be having the time of her life.

Beneath the VR goggles, Carson felt like an eagle as he swooped through the trees. His fingers lightly touched the controls, but the ground beneath his feet seemed to melt away as he became immersed. He imagined he could even feel the breeze on his face. . .

Soon, the day to travel to London was upon them. As promised, Kay assured her brother that she'd cover for them all. Carson left a note for his dad informing him that he was at Eddie's. He gave Kay's phone number but doubted his dad would bother calling to check.

However, the shock came when they arrived at the train station to find Kay standing with a backpack over one shoulder and her mobile phone in the other. She gave them a casual wave and turned her attention back to her phone.

"About time you showed up."

Carson shook both fists in the air and silently mouthed *what the heck?* to Eddie, who looked utterly bewildered. He coughed and tried to sound as casual as possible.

"Oh, hi, sis. Going somewhere?"

Kay didn't look up from her phone. "London, aren't we?"

"That's . . . unexpected."

Kay gave them all a withering sidelong glance. "You don't think I was going to let you twerps go on your own, right? I mean, why should you get all the fun?"

Eddie glanced between Trix and Carson's worried expressions and shrugged: what could he do?

Kay started walking to the platform. "And don't sweat it. I'm not coming to your crummy flyee-thing. I've got friends I'm gonna meet up with."

"Maybe this won't be so bad after all?" said Trix as they followed her to the platform.

With Vanta tucked in Carson's backpack, the train journey proved to be uneventful. Carson's worries about having Kay with them ebbed away and he settled down to enjoy the trip. The posh hotel was not far from the station, and checking in was simple. To their surprise they had been given a multi-bedroom suite. Even Kay was impressed, and spent several minutes posting selfies on every social media site she could.

Breaking the Coke out from the minibar, they all raised their glasses to thank Marcus Nation for such a generous gift.

Bathed in the soft pulsing glow from Vanta as she recharged, Carson found himself more excited than he had been for a long time. He could just imagine the smile on his mum's face, how pleased she would have been for him. Tomorrow, he'd try his best for her. . .

Chapter 16
THE UK FINALS

Kay left the hotel early to meet her friends, armed with promises from Eddie, Trix and Carson that they would meet her at Euston Station in good time to catch the train home. After checking out of the hotel, an electric MPV minivan was waiting outside for them. The rather sleepy-looking driver flashed a card with "Carsonators" written on it and beckoned them inside.

"We've finally made it to the big leagues!" grinned Carson as they headed to the racing venue.

Eddie gave a low whistle as they stepped through the arena entrance. "This was not how I imagined it at all!"

Trix grunted in agreement as she looked across the semi-final course. Carson cradled his backpack in both arms, allowing Vanta to peek out of the open zipper.

It was not a real stadium, but it had been cleverly put together around the docks using several permanent buildings, fences and a specially erected grandstand. The track was larger than the last one, built on the edge of the water. To one side, rows of tiered seating had been set up, complete with camera platforms to televise the event. Parts of the course were elevated high into the air with obstacles suspended from cranes, while others floated on the water and, as far as Carson could make out, they would have to fly into the hull of an old 1960s battleship and out the other side. The audience was shielded from the course by massive plastic screens that lined the perimeter.

A young woman in a Constructor League T-shirt greeted them at the entrance and checked their details on her tablet before escorting them to the racing paddock. It was already filled with teams from across the country preparing their drones. There was a wide assortment of machines, some as sleek as darts, others armed to the teeth.

Carson spotted a shimmer of red hair. India was talking to her parents as they assembled Sixtus on the bench. She glanced around and stared at him. A smile spread across Carson's face and he waved. India scowled and looked sharply away. Carson's awkward fail was interrupted by Trix nudging him in the ribs.

"Over there..." she muttered. The AirBlitz team were hunched over their machine, which had clearly been modified with a weapon strapped underneath. "Maybe we should have thought of that?"

Carson gingerly placed Vanta on the table. She looked the same as ever. "I think we'll be OK."

"Carsonators!" Marcus Nation's booming voice made them all look up. He was wearing the same combo of Hawaiian shirt and shorts, but this time with Day-Glo green trainers, making him look like an explosion in a rainbow factory. "You got here!"

Carson shook his hand. "Well, thanks to you."

Nation paused, then gestured around. "This is what I do. A league needs its underdogs and you seemed to catch everybody's imagination last time."

"Underdogs?" Eddie sounded offended. He pointed to himself. "Us?"

Marcus Nation laughed and patted him on the shoulder. "You bet. You should've had your schedule emailed to you, right? You have been allocated ten minutes for a sight lap so you get to know the course, and I should warn you this is the most difficult I have ever seen, and we've been doing this all around the world."

Despite Vanta's capabilities, Carson was beginning to feel nervous.

Nation continued: "Then when the crowds arrive you'll all have a hot lap, all the drones out there together, it'll be awesome. Positions will be based on your qualifying speeds from the last event. Then we're into the big race. This time there will only be a single race. Ten whole laps, so it'll test the endurance on your batteries. Winner becomes the first-ever Constructor League UK champ! Then off to the finals. Next two runners-up get to go too."

Nation's voice dropped in volume. "And you should know who the favourites are."

Carson, Eddie and Trix exchanged thrilled looks.

Marcus Nation smiled ... then nodded to another bench where Logan46 stood, their bodies shielding the drone they were working on. "Those guys. I'd watch your backs if I were you."

He snapped his fingers and pointed at them, then zeroed in on another team. Carson felt crushed.

"That was the worst pep talk in the history of pep," sighed Trix.

If anything, if made Carson feel more determined than ever. UK champions? Yeah, he'd like that...

Vanta's first sprint around the track was not as difficult as Carson had feared. He took it slow, despite Vanta insisting on going flat out. The sighting lap enabled him to get a feel for each turn and sudden climb – one of which was vertically straight up, a difficult thing for any drone to do at speed. Only when he was skimming over the water did Vanta give her first complaint.

"Don't get too low," she warned. "I can do a lot, but I can't swim."

Next was a sharp turn into the battleship. This would be a high-speed race through claustrophobic narrow corridors, down a steel stairwell and along even narrower passageways before exiting. Pipes hanging from the ceiling and irregular steel walls made formidable obstacles: a badly timed overtake would be disastrous.

The other racers would try to watch one another's sight laps, hoping to see any potential disadvantage in their competitors. That was Eddie's job; sitting, eating crisps and watching laps was something he excelled in. As soon as Vanta had landed back in the paddock, he ran over to them, gasping for breath.

"Those AirBlitz fellas were paying special attention to you out there," he gasped.

Carson looked around but couldn't see them. "Did you hear them say anything?"

"No, but they took some photos and kept muttering to each other."

For the first time since they arrived, Carson felt apprehensive. It felt as if he should be avoiding everybody. All day he had tried to avoid India, although he had watched Sixtus as it soared around the course. In addition, he had made sure he was never in the same place as the Logan46 team, who appeared to scowl at every opportunity. Now he thought about it, Terry in the AirBlitz team certainly matched the size of the male intruder in his house . . . but it didn't make sense. What would they gain by trying to break in? Why bother trying to sabotage the Carsonators? After all, even Marcus Nation referred to them as the underdogs; if they didn't compete, somebody else would fill their place.

The hours of the sighting laps quickly passed, with every team member constantly tweaking their drones. All except the Carsonators.

"How's your battery level?" Trix asked as she ran a gentle brush over Vanta's propellers.

"Maximum!"

"It would help if I could see all your readings on my iPad. That's supposed to be part of my job."

"I can handle it all."

Trix tossed the cleaning cloth on to the table. "Well, so much for my pre-race checklist. You're going to put me out of a job as engineer."

Eddie returned after stuffing himself with hot dogs as he watched the other teams practise.

"I reckon the Scottish Highlands team are going to be our toughest opponent. They're even better than Logan46."

"Anybody else we should be looking out for?" Trix asked.

Eddie shrugged. "I suppose so. . ."

Trix waited expectantly, but Eddie shrugged again. Finally, Trix sighed. "Well, that's the sort of insightful observation that makes us the best."

"It's AirBlitz I'm worried about," Carson said as he watched the team gather around their drone. He shared his suspicions about the break-in as the seats filled up with spectators from around the country. The Scottish supporters raised the volume with boisterous cheering as they unfurled a huge St Andrew's Cross over several rows of empty seats. They sat together despite the fact there were three regional teams from Scotland who had qualified. The noise increased as the north-west regional fans arrived and began drumming the floor with their feet. The south-western supporters, mostly from Devon and Cornwall, arrived in a flurry of brightly coloured banners with their team, Speed-Rager, emblazoned across. Bright flashing lights on top of the banners added to the growing kaleidoscope.

More banners and increasing noise added to the excitement. The various fans sang out competing chants, stomping the floor and clapping, but somehow it all worked and sounded melodic and friendly.

"There must be a thousand of them!" said Carson.

"The seating capacity is for five thousand people, and they're sold out," Vanta replied.

Eddie frowned. "How do you know that?"

"I may have hacked into their website." Vanta at least had the decency to *sound* guilty.

"That's a lot of people watching," Carson muttered, suddenly feeling very nervous. A league assistant passed through the paddock telling the racers to get ready for the hot lap.

"Here we go," said Eddie, clapping his hands enthusiastically. He carefully picked Vanta up as Trix gathered their equipment and they headed for the launch pads.

"Hey, Carson?" whispered Vanta conspiratorially.

"Yeah?"

"Let's win this thing."

Chapter 16
GET SET... RACE!

The hot lap was supposed to be civilized. The twenty-five participating drones were set in order, their positions based on their times in the regional events. They would make one lap around the race at a slow, steady speed so the audience could get a good look at them all. There would be no overtaking, no bumping or hitting.

And for the most part it *was* civilized, giving the audience a chance to cheer on their favourites.

Vanta had started from the middle of the pack. Carson had been disappointed when Eddie had informed him that their qualification time from the previous heat had been nothing short of average. Out in the open, the other racers respected the rules. . . But as soon as the drones entered tunnels and the tight passageways inside the battleship, they veered towards each other in sneaky attempts to drift an opponent into the wall. Carson wasn't falling for such devious tricks. He was also guided by Trix, who observed Vanta's point of view on her tablet, although she didn't have the 3D experience Carson did through the VR goggles. Trix also kept glancing at the action broadcast on the jumbo screens to spot any problems ahead. She wanted to keep Vanta out of harm's way, despite the drone's constant stream of threats.

"I should clip his blades!" she growled. "Oh, come near me again, pal, and you're toast!"

Once or twice, Carson could feel Vanta try to wrest control back.

"No, you don't, Vanta. Stay with me."

Eddie, however, wasn't watching the drones; his eyes were on the other teams, especially AirBlitz. As the venue filled to capacity and the noise from the audience grew, he became increasingly anxious.

The teams' paddock area was set up outside a

building that was used as a canteen for the behind-the-scenes team and the racers. Eddie kept an eye out for anyone acting suspicious. It was only when he noticed a fluorescent-green-jacketed security guard glaring suspiciously at him that he realized *he* was the one acting suspicious.

The long summer evening drew on, but that didn't stop the track from illuminating in bright neon. Poles throughout the course that Eddie hadn't even noticed suddenly exploded into fountains of flames, and smoke drifted strategically over the course, all adding further obstacles that hadn't been there moments earlier.

Now Carson and Vanta had begun the hot lap, Eddie had nothing to do. He quickly checked his sister's social media feeds to see she was busy all over London posting selfies with her friends.

So far, so good, he thought. Glancing up from his phone he noticed two figures in black suits keeping to the edge of the paddock. A bearded man and a woman with bobbed blonde hair, both wearing dark glasses and looking very out of place amongst the scruffy drone teams. They appeared more interested in the teams than the race itself. A dozen more identically suited figures patrolled the stadium. *Security,* he assumed. Although he did wonder what they were being kept secure from.

Eddie watched one of the giant monitor screens as Marcus Nation warmed up the crowd to fever pitch, selling the UK final for all it was worth.

"As our racers complete the hot lap, it's time to tell you about a surprise they have no idea is coming. Aside from the traps and pitfalls across the course, we have one extra deadly element: the *Dodge Droooone!*"

With that, a hatch on the battleship's deck slid open and a huge, ten-rotored drone swooped into view. It was the size of a coffee table, its front shaped like a plough blade that curved to a sharp point.

"What's going on?" asked Carson. He could hear the announcement, but all he could see was Vanta's point of view as they slalomed through a set of flaming poles. He could tell a few of the pilots ahead had become distracted, as they almost flew straight into the fire.

"Trust me, you don't want to know," Trix muttered as she marked the position of the newcomer on her iPad.

"The *Dodge Droooone —*" Nation sounded as if

he was introducing a wrestler "– is completely on autopilot and will be going *in the opposite direction* from our racers. Let me tell you, a head-on collision with this dude and it's bye-bye!"

The crowd whooped and cheered.

"I really don't like these people," Vanta sighed.

Eddie watched the Dodge Drone growl through the sky, accompanied by mutters and gasps from the other competitors. He patted Carson on the shoulder.

"Good luck, mate."

Trix's eyes never left the course. "Eddie, can you move to the other end of the paddock and get a better view on that Dodge Drone? I'm a little blind here."

"Sure. I'll vid-chat you," he said, thankful for having something to do. He hurried past the other teams, who all ignored him. Standing on an empty metal flight case somebody had left around, Eddie had a clearer view of the arena.

"...GET SET – RACE!" yelled Nation as the starting buzzer echoed across the docks.

Eddie picked out the Dodge Drone and readied his phone to vid-chat Trix, but then hesitated when he noticed the two nearby suited figures were acting oddly. The bearded man now had a small device in his hand and was holding it towards the drones.

His heart began to thump in his chest as thoughts of sabotage rattled through his head. He spotted a security guard walking through the paddock and considered warning him, but of what? The duo hadn't actually done anything, plus the guard had seen them and walked on, so they were obviously supposed to be there. . .

"Yahooooo!" Vanta hollered as she undertook another drone as they flew around a tight curve.

Carson felt a thrill too as the drone receded in his rear-view screen. The first half of the lap had been a morass of bumping and nudging, which he had somehow managed to keep Vanta clear of. A drone in front of him had succumbed to a surprise attack when another racer from Wales, Dragon Fly, had swooped down and plucked the drone from the air with a powerful pair of claws mounted in its undercarriage. A quick snip had torn the drone in half – much to the delight of the crowd.

Carson was feeling tense. "Where's that Dodge Drone?"

"Hold on. . ." Trix looked around but couldn't see Eddie. She tried to vid-call him, but he didn't answer. "Where the heck is he?"

"Talk to me, Trix."

She looked at the map on her iPad. The dot she had set up depicting the Dodge Drone was closing in on Vanta, although it was nothing more than a guess. The drone could have sped up, slowed or even changed course. "It's about fifteen seconds ahead of you," she warned him. "Vanta, do you see it yet?"

"My sensors are picking out too many moving obstacles," Vanta said. "I can't tell which is which!"

Carson's hand was trembling at the thought of what lurked ahead. He didn't have to wait long.

His pack of racers had just emerged from a tunnel and were zooming low towards the canal. Ahead, a series of solid horizontal concrete spars cut across the course, each decreasing in height to force the racers closer to the water; it was the section Vanta was most apprehensive about.

During the descent, the drone swarm suddenly scattered in every direction. Carson barely had time to jink to the right as a racer in front of him hit the Dodge Drone head-on. There was an explosion and Vanta was pelted with plastic parts and bits of molten circuit boards. Carson managed to roll upside down – nearly scraping the Dodge's undercarriage.

In the blink of an eye, Carson turned Vanta the correct way up just as they reached the water. Ahead, the leading drones kicked up wakes in the still canal water. He tried to accclerate, but the controls didn't respond properly and two drones seized the opportunity to overtake them.

"What's wrong?" Trix asked urgently. "Your power seems down."

"I'm not sure . . . there was a power flux. I think something struck my aft-port blade." Vanta sounded worried.

"Back left," Trix translated before Carson could ask. "Did some of wrecked drone strike you?"

Carson had a sinking feeling in his gut. As they circled around to cross the line for the first lap he was already falling back in the pack. A broken rotor would be the end of the race for them. And they still had another nine laps to go.

Chapter 17
NOT IN CONTROL

Eddie edged closer to the two suspicious characters so he could overhear the bearded man as he read the screen on the device in his hand.

"Syncrone readings match the target. It's out there, but I don't see..."

Eddie suddenly became aware the man was looking straight at him. His eyes narrowed with suspicion. Eddie knew he should just act innocent, as if he hadn't heard a thing... but he was terrible at acting innocent.

Instead he suddenly turned and ran.

The woman didn't hesitate. She broke into a sprint and charged after him.

Eddie wasn't thinking as he ran towards the canteen building. As he passed through the door he suddenly realized what a silly move he'd made: everybody was outside. He would be trapped and alone!

Carson almost flew straight into a wall as Vanta suddenly accelerated, overtaking three drones in quick succession as they whizzed through blazing hoops.

"Wow! What was that?" he blurted as he managed to steer Vanta back on course.

"I don't know," said Vanta. "My power came back online. Everything seems OK now."

Trix wasn't convinced. "Are you sure you're not hurt? I mean, damaged?"

"I don't think so."

"Good. In that case, look ahead: the Dodge Drone is coming up again!"

Vanta shot into the battleship. The grey walls became a blur as she accelerated even faster than before.

"Carson, be careful."

"I don't know where all this power is coming from."

Vanta had an answer for that. "The problem we had with the radio controller seems to have cleared up."

Neither of them could see the frown on Trix's face. She had fixed drones, made robotic arms and patched up numerous laptops often enough to know that electrical components never repaired themselves. It was always a warning that something worse was about to happen. But right now, she was staring at her iPad.

"Here it comes!"

Vanta was just about to drop down the battleship staircase when the Dodge Drone powered up towards her. There was only a narrow gap between the massive aircraft and the ceiling and Carson guided Vanta straight for it.

A second later, a flat drone, resembling a flying saucer, bashed into Vanta as it made for the same gap. Carson recalled the sighting laps and remembered this one was called Wolverine. In the paddocks the Scottish lads flying it were always laughing and sharing jokes with anybody who'd listen – but right now they were out for blood.

Carson nudged the stick to ram Vanta into

Wolverine – only noticing at the last second that the edge of the saucer had a spinning blade rotating around it.

Vanta would be sliced in half!

Carson wasn't sure what happened next; it all occurred in seconds. One moment they were on a collision course, the next there was a crackle of electricity and lightning arced between Vanta and Wolverine. The lethal flying saucer suddenly lost power and dropped into the path of the Dodge Drone. Vanta was suddenly through the gap, leaving the sound of tearing metal and plastic behind.

Trix had been watching everything on her screen. "What was that?"

"Something must've short-circuited," Vanta muttered.

Carson had the feeling that maybe he wasn't completely in control of this race...

Eddie ran through the empty canteen, desperately looking for a place to hide. The woman was gaining on him with the speed of a professional athlete. He pushed through a door and into a zigzagging breeze block corridor that led to the toilets. He noticed the door to a storage closet was partially ajar and threw himself inside, crashing against the mops stored within. He yanked the door closed, plunging himself into darkness and causing dozens of spare toilet rolls to cascade on him from the shelf above. He just hoped his pursuer hadn't heard.

He heard running footsteps pass by. The sound of leather soles on polished concrete shuffled to a stop a little further down the corridor.

THUMP-THUMP-THUMP – Eddie was terrified his heart would betray him. Despite the summer heat, he shivered.

The silence from outside was beginning to worry him. Had she gone? How long should he stay inside? Just as he considered leaving, he heard her voice.

"Agent Bevan, I've lost the target. Has he doubled back?" He didn't hear the reply, but was relieved when she said, "OK. I'm heading back."

In the darkness, Eddie felt smug at giving the woman the slip.

Then the closet suddenly lit up as the phone he was holding in his hand illuminated with a text message from his sister – and an accompanying chime broke the stillness, betraying his hiding place.

The closet door suddenly opened and Eddie spilled out with the toilet rolls. The woman stared down at him and pressed one finger against a small earpiece.

"Target acquired."

The race wasn't just a test of endurance for the drones; it was taking its toll on the pilots too.

This course was the longest Carson had ever raced in a single go. With the heat of the day and tight-fitting VR goggles, he was sweating heavily and his mouth was parched. He hoped the other racers were feeling the same.

A drone just behind him wobbled erratically, probably under the unsteady hands of its tired pilot. The fourth lap was relatively uneventful, with the racers now falling into rhythm – no longer eager to scrap, but just keen to see it through to the end of the race. It took another lap before Trix had found a bottle of water and poured it into Carson's mouth. Most of it ran down his top, but he was thankful: what he did drink perked up his attention.

"The wall" was coming up, a thirty-metre vertical climb that strained every drone's engines, and was designed to slow them down as it became a test of vertical, not horizontal, speed. Fortunately, Vanta had the ability to twist her rotors parallel to the ground, elegantly powering herself upward. It was a feature that Marcus Nation pointed out to the crowd in a surprised tone.

Above, Carson saw smoke pouring from a rival's motor as the blades overheated. Before they had even reached the top, the drone's engines caught fire and the limp machine suddenly plummeted towards Vanta. Carson banked around it and watched the rear-view as it splashed down in the cold water below. Then they were suddenly over the wall.

"There are twelve racers left," said Trix as they began their sixth lap. "And we're in the middle. 'Could do better', to quote Eddie's last school report."

With each racer taken out of the race, the crowd had cheered and stomped their feet. Action replays of the destruction kept looping on the screens, although most had been too quick to capture on video.

"Another drink would be good," said Carson, licking his lips.

Trix looked around to tell Eddie but couldn't see him anywhere. *Typical*, she thought, *he's never around when you need him.*

Eddie tried to stand, but a strong hand pushed him back into his chair. The bearded man, now identified as Agent Bevan, had joined Eddie and the as yet nameless blonde woman in the canteen. As they leaned down to his eye level, Eddie noticed they both had pistols holstered under their jackets, but these were angular with sharp edges, and looked more menacing than guns he'd seen on TV.

"You know you can't do this," Eddie said with more bravery than he felt.

Bevan examined Eddie's phone. "You will be surprised at what we can do, son."

"I'll find out which team you're helping cheat, then you've all had it!"

The man's eyebrows rose and he smiled in disbelief. "Cheat? Is that what you think we're doing?"

Eddie deflated with uncertainty. "Well, um, it was. . ." he mumbled.

Bevan held up Eddie's phone. "You want to tell me your passcode?"

Eddie shook his head. The man smiled and tossed the phone to the women. "Agent Anders, you know what to do."

"Bevan and Anders?" Eddie tried to sound braver than he sounded. "You sound like a really rubbish music act."

Agent Anders suddenly grabbed his hand and forced it against the phone. It unlocked. He tried to look around to see what she was doing, but the pacing man captured his attention with a snap of his fingers.

"What team are you with?"

Eddie knew it was stupid to answer. Bevan seemed to appreciate his courage. He stopped pacing and peered at Eddie with steely grey eyes.

"Look, son, we know you're with one of those teams out there. Our agents have infiltrated every home to find what we're looking for. We could easily arrest you all. . ."

Eddie's face scrunched in confusion. "Arrest? We haven't done anything. . ." but he was rapidly putting a picture together, and right in the middle of that scene was Vanta. He guessed that arresting every team would draw too much attention to the agents' activities. He decided his best defence at the moment was ignorance.

"I'll ask you one more time, son. Then things will get ... *complicated*." The threat was obvious and drew the corner of the man's lips up in a cold smile. "What. Team?"

Eddie closed his eyes in defeat. He exhaled a long sigh. "AirBlitz." It was little more than a whisper.

Bevan looked sharply at Anders, who was still behind Eddie. "They were the fastest in their local heat," he heard her say.

"But their drone doesn't look like right. None of them do!"

"Shape-shifting adaptive camouflage," Anders reminded him.

Eddie had no idea what they were talking about. His gaze was drawn to six people entering the canteen. He recognized them as the south-west team, Speed-Rager, and, judging by their expressions, they'd lost their aircraft.

"Don't say anything," Bevan quietly warned him.

"Hey, Speed-Ragers!" Eddie shouted as loud as

he could, jumping to his feet. "Bad luck out there!" From their scowls it was clear they were not in a chatty mood, but they drew closer. He noticed the two agents either side of him exchange looks and tense, but they didn't move to restrain him. "My uncle here was betting you guys would easily win! Isn't the right, unc?" Eddie playfully elbowed Bevan in the ribs with force. "In fact, he was just placing a bet. See?"

Eddie snatched his phone from Bevan's hand and flashed it up in a quick motion so that the Speed-Ragers couldn't actually see the screen.

"Too bad," said one of the team in a soft West Country accent. "That stupid Dodge Drone was what got us. Next year we'll be back and ready. Bet on us then, mate."

Eddie smiled brightly. "You hear that, unc? Next year you can put your life savings on these boys and finally afford that hip replacement! Oh well! I better get back to the race!"

He shoved through the group – casually pushing one of the teenagers in between him and Anders as she reached out to stop him.

"Sorry! Better luck next time!" shouted Eddie as

he ran for the paddock. The agents, desperate not to cause a fuss, still hadn't moved to follow.

He now had only one thing on his mind: he had to warn his friends.

Chapter 18
ALL TO PLAY FOR

"Lap eight and all to play for!" whooped Marcus Nation. "And we are down to nine racers in what has turned out to be glorious havoc!"

The crowd responded with a massive roar of approval.

Carson wasn't listening. He had other worries on his mind.

"Oh no."

"What? What is it?" Trix asked urgently, scanning her iPad for any signs of trouble.

Carson didn't answer. AirBlitz, Wolverine and Logan46 were in the lead and evenly matched in speed, so now it came down to brute force to knock the competition out. Up ahead was Sixtus – and a pair of drones were moving in on her.

The north-east team's drone, Killer Driller, inched above Sixtus. A moment later Carson understood the real meaning of the racer's name as a spinning drill bit lowered from the fuselage – straight for the radio receiver on Sixtus. If that was knocked out, India would have no control at all.

"We've got to help her!"

"Why?" both Trix and Vanta asked at the same time.

"She is our enemy," Vanta reminded him.

"I think enemy is a strong word—" Carson began, but then yelped as the second drone, the Hibernian Monster, ferociously broadsided Vanta.

Vanta veered sideways – a hair's breadth from colliding with the wall. "Why you little *helicopter!*" she spat.

Carson felt Vanta bank towards the aggressive drone – and he wasn't pushing on the control sticks.

"Vanta!"

"Sorry, I'm not very good at insults."

"I mean the control – give it back! Now!"

With a huff, he felt the control snap back to him and he prevented Vanta from exacting revenge.

"We can't let him get away with that!" Vanta shouted down his ear.

Carson had no intention of letting that happen.

"Get me over it and on my command, flip me under!" Vanta instructed.

Carson positioned Vanta over the Hibernian Monster. He didn't see a steel lasso tow cable extend from Vanta's belly hatch – but Trix saw it all on the monitors. The lasso tightened around the Scottish drone's antenna array.

"Now!" barked Vanta.

Carson acrobatically flipped her in a barrel roll. The cable pulled tight and swung the Hibernian Monster around, smashing it against Killer Driller like a wrecking ball!

The Hibernian Monster was impaled on Killer Driller and both drones spun out of control into the wall with a terminal impact.

Trix yelled with delight and Carson heard Marcus Nation and the crowd respond with whoops of appreciation – apart from the north-east fans, who booed loudly.

Nation bellowed across the arena: "And the underdog takes two down for the price of one!"

Carson was watching the rear-view screen with a smug smile when he heard Vanta call out: "CARSON!"

His concentration flicked back ahead just as the Dodge Drone loomed into view. Sixtus banked at the last moment – one of her propellers shattering against the massive drone. She wobbled but stayed in control.

Carson wasn't so quick.

It felt as if his fingers had knotted together as he fumbled the controls. Before Vanta had even responded to the moves, he knew he'd miscalculated.

The front of Vanta tilted up – but not the back, as if she was pulling a wheelie in the air. Vanta's raised nose cleared the plough blade – but her tail clipped the edge of it. Then two things happened instantaneously:

They shot out of the tunnel and found themselves thirty metres up in the air. And at the very same moment, Vanta lost all power to her motors and plunged straight down, spinning like a merry-go-round, towards the water.

*

Eddie ran at full pelt from the building, and straight into the Killer Driller team, who were furious, screaming at one another in thick Geordie accents. He instinctively started towards Trix and Carson, who also seemed to be yelling.

He glanced behind and saw the agents were following him. At the last moment, Eddie veered aside and ran towards the AirBlitz team. Luckily, they were too immersed in the race to notice him as he stopped and watched their screens alongside them. He risked a look behind and saw his pursuers were lurking in the shadows of the doorway and they made no attempt to come closer.

Until the race ended, he was safe.

Carson still had full video connectivity with Vanta as she spiralled out of control. It was so intense that a wave of dizziness overcame him and he staggered sideways.

Trix lunged in an attempt to keep him upright but failed and they both toppled to the ground.

"What's wrong with you?"

Carson tried to answer, but his senses were convincing him he was spinning out of control towards the canal. His only answer was to throw up over Trix!

"URGH!" she screamed, hitting him in the arm – before the vile smell struck her and she forcibly pushed him away.

Vanta suddenly managed to kick her engines back in motion and the horrible spinning stopped. Carson still had the controller in a vice-like grip. Even with the world spinning around him, he had the sense to pull back the controls.

Out on the course, Vanta skimmed the canal. A curtain of water rose up behind her – then she leapt into the air with a "YAHHOOO!!!"

Carson was still on his hands and knees, the VR headset pushed against the ground as he fought sickness. The crowd watched Vanta wobble back into the race, faster than ever. Carson didn't even notice that she overtook Sixtus as they crossed the line...

"The final lap!" declared Marcus Nation.

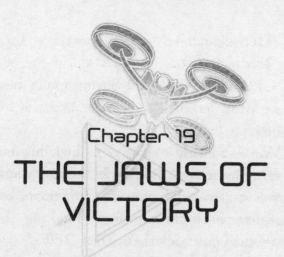

Chapter 19
THE JAWS OF VICTORY

The sick feeling was starting to ease. However, the lingering smell of vomit made Carson feel queasy again. Trix yanked his arm to pull him upright.

"Last lap, idiot! Focus!" she ordered. She had unzipped her pukey jacket and thrown it aside, deliberately towards the Logan46 team. It took a moment for them to start reacting to the odour.

Carson's legs were shaking and his hands and brow felt cold and clammy. "I don't know if I can do this."

"We're in third." Trix's jaw clenched in an effort to remain calm. "We could actually win."

"I feel dizzy. . ."

"Then let me take the final lap."

Carson considered it. She not only fixed the drones, she was an excellent pilot too. But then it wouldn't be *his* race. . .

"Or let me," chimed in Vanta hopefully.

The controls felt like jelly in his trembling hands. Worse, Sixtus, with only five functional engines, suddenly moved past him.

"Fourth place," sighed Trix. "You're snatching defeat from the jaws of victory."

Carson felt sick again, but not from motion, from the fact he knew it was all over for him. Letting Vanta take over was against the rules, and it would get them disqualified. They had made it this far on his piloting abilities, and even if they could convincingly fake controlling her, he cursed the sense of pride that Eddie had drummed into him: what was the point in winning if you had to cheat at it?

A memory burst into his mind: a snowy evening several years ago, when he had been playing an old board game with his parents, one of his dad's favourites – Risk. His mum had caught him cheating and then lectured him on the spirit of sportsmanship.

At the time he had just felt annoyed at being caught, but now he understood her disappointment.

But not cheating didn't leave him with many options other than to lose.

Or let Trix try.

He was sure there was nothing in the rules about swapping pilots mid-race.

With a heartfelt sigh, he nodded. "OK, Trix, let's do this. There's a straight coming up. . ." He felt her unfasten the straps on his VR headset with one hand while holding it against his eyes with the other. "NOW!"

The sudden removal of the headset mid-race made Carson think he had jumped bodies. And in a way he had. Once moment he was soaring towards the flaming slalom section, six metres in the air – the next he was standing still in the bullpen. He staggered as he lost his balance.

Trix smoothly put the helmet on, holding it in place with one hand, the other blindly groping in the air. "The controller!"

Carson thrust the controller into her hand, then pulled the helmet straps on tight. That was it; Trix was piloting. He looked around for Eddie and was surprised to see him standing with the AirBlitz team. What the heck was he doing over there?

A change in pitch from the audience made him look up at the screen. Trix was accelerating past Sixtus and had Logan46 and AirBlitz in her sights as they zoomed into the battleship for the very last time.

He looked around for Trix's iPad, spotting it on the floor. He picked it up just in time to see Vanta had passed the Dodge Drone. Then the lead four drones were back out of the battleship and the arena cameras picked them out.

"The controls are still interfering with Vanta's power," he warned Trix. "You can't outrun them. Unless we can slow them down we might just hang in for third."

Trix grit her teeth. "Third? I don't think so."

Vanta started to make violent zigzags and Carson feared there was another engine problem until he heard Trix laughing. She was deliberately rushing towards AirBlitz and Logan46 to make them think she was going to ram them, before pulling away at the last moment.

"What are you doing?"

"You gave me an idea!"

Carson watched as both rivals quickly banked to avoid her – any collisions now could put them out of the game. But the simple act of jerking sideways made them slow down just a little … and Carson suddenly saw the genius in Trix's plan.

Vanta raced between them like a missile. AirBlitz has lost so much speed that Sixtus suddenly nudged into third place as they turned into the final straight.

The entire stadium was on their feet in the last few seconds as Marcus Nation's voice became an almost incoherent scream:

"And the underdogs win! Logan46 … and Sixtus snatching third place! Oh my gosh! Oh my gosh! Who would have thought that from the underdogs?"

Trix bounced on the spot, shrieking with delight. "We did it! We did it!" She guided Vanta down to the team's feet in a quick landing and tore off the goggles. Laughing with glee, she hugged Carson and the two of them jumped up and down.

Carson smiled, but inside he felt a little jealous that he hadn't been the one crossing the finishing line.

"Where's Eddie?" Trix asked, looking around as the paddock became a hive of activity.

Carson scooped up Vanta, holding her carefully. Despite the action, her engines were cool and her chassis showed no signs of damage.

"How are you?" he asked in a low voice.

"Amazing! They love me!" she replied brightly, her camera darting this way and that to take in the jubilant crowd.

There was a flurry of movement on the far side and, to everybody's surprise, the AirBlitz team were being forcibly escorted out by a dozen stern-looking black suits. They overheard fragments of accusations about *cheating* and *match fixing*. Eddie appeared at their side, his face pale and eyes darting around fearfully.

"Did you see that?" screamed Trix. "We won!"

Eddie gave a weak smile but was in no mood to celebrate. "Yeah. Great. Well done..." then he saw the goggles were around Trix's neck. "You were flying?"

"Only the last lap, but ... we won!"

Carson finally registered the apprehension on his friend's face. "What happened?"

"Let's just say we need to get out of here as fast as possible." Before he could say any more, Marcus

Nation and a gaggle of assistants hurried towards them. He pointed at them and winked.

"You guys! I knew you'd do it!"

"Really?" said Carson, raising a sceptical eyebrow. "Only 'underdogs' didn't sound so supportive."

Nation flashed a charming smile and raised an eyebrow. "It made you fly for your lives, didn't it?" He nodded over to see the last of the suits disappear through the door. "And lucky those dudes from the racing commission spotted those cheats." "

"How did they cheat?" Trix asked nervously, her eyes flicking between Nation and Vanta.

Marcus Nation waved his hand dismissively. "Oh, radio jammers or something. That's not really important. What's important is you guys!" He pointed both index fingers at them like imaginary pistols. "Bam! Bam! You were on fire!" He whirled the trio around to pose for the mass of cameras. "That was awesome!"

"You said they were from the racing commission?" said Eddie dubiously.

Nation kept his smile fixed in place as he nodded. "Yup. To be taken seriously as a league we had to have the CIAM involved."

Trix and Carson swapped blank looks.

"The Comité International d'Aéromodelisme," said Eddie while forcing a smile. He noticed his friends looking at him in surprise. "What? I'm supposed to know these things, aren't I? I am the manager," he added loudly for the cameras. He turned to Nation. "And just to double check – we have won the prize money?"

Marcus Nation laughed. "Oh, sure. That will be wired to your account. But what's better than that is you're the official, the *first*, UK Constructor League champions! Well done! That means you're representing the UK in Seoul!"

Carson frowned. "Seoul?"

"The capital of South Korea! That's where we're holding the world championship, dummy!"

The shriek of joy from Trix deafened Carson.

The next two hours were a blur of congratulations. Some of the racers shook their hands, others just scowled. The league assistants guided them to a podium, where the Carsonators were announced as the winners. The Logan46 team took second, but that didn't seem to please them at all. From the way they were staring at Carson, he wouldn't have been surprised if they shot laser beams at him from their eyes.

However, he was pleasantly surprised to see India standing on the third-place podium. She was beaming with pride and waving to the crowd. Then followed several minutes in front of the TV cameras, during which Carson was thankful Eddie did most of the talking. He was enjoying his moment in the limelight and mentioned as often as he could how he kept the team on their toes and in tiptop condition. He was asked repeatedly to show their winning drone, which he kept refusing. It was only after Marcus Nation gave them a stern nod – and a reluctant shrug from Carson – that Eddie pulled Vanta from his pack to show her off.

To his surprise, her upswept arms holding the propellers now sagged low and angled backwards and her fuselage looked fatter, giving her a strikingly different appearance. Carson restrained his gasp and noticed his friends' puzzled expressions. Held in his hands, he could feel surges of power flowing through the little drone, causing her chassis to quiver with delight. Luckily, Vanta didn't start talking in front of the cameras.

The circus was finally over, and they found themselves being led down a concrete tunnel with the other two teams, to the loading area where electric MPV people carriers were waiting to take them to the train station. Marcus Nation told them that all the details about the final would be emailed to them, and the flights taken care of, but they had to make sure they were ready for the following weekend.

The Logan46 team climbed into their waiting vehicle without a word. Running a hand through his short, spiky hair, Logan himself roughly shouldered past Carson and muttered under his breath. "You're dead meat next time."

Trix and Eddie climbed into the next people carrier, but Carson stopped when he felt a tap on his shoulder. It was India, nervously wringing her hands.

"I wanted to say thank you for what you did on that eighth lap. You saved my bacon. I think I misjudged you."

"No problem." He felt suddenly buoyant. But

the feeling quickly disappeared when India's smile broadened.

"But I'm going to totally destroy you when I see you in Korea." She skipped towards the last MPV, where her parents were waiting for her.

Bewildered, Carson climbed into his vehicle and they pulled away. Eddie nudged his friend in the arm.

"What did your girlfriend say?"

"That she was going to totally destroy me next time she sees me," said Carson flatly.

Chapter 20
EVASION!

The drive to the station began in stops and starts as the silent electric minivan joined the choked London roads. The Carsonators were assigned the same driver who had picked them up from the hotel, and he hadn't said a word, seeming content to listen to a dull political show on the radio. Carson, Eddie and Trix had sat right at the back.

Eddie messaged his sister they were on their way to the train station, then tried to settle back and relax. His heart was still hammering from the encounter with the agents, and he kept nervously glancing behind them and drumming his fingers on his knees.

The smile hadn't left Trix's face as she scrutinized their trophy. It was an old circuit board shaped into the outline of a drone. Carson stared into the middle distance.

"Thanks, Carson." He was surprised when Trix tapped him with the trophy. "I know you really wanted to be the one crossing the line, but we had to switch."

He nodded, trying to hide just how gutted he felt. "I know. You were brilliant. Besides, we're a team. We all won. What does it matter who was flying?"

"We're being followed," Eddie said urgently. He unfastened his seat belt so he could twist around and peer out of the back window.

The other two looked at him in alarm – then burst into laughter.

"Maybe it's a crazy fan?" Trix said in a scary voice.

"He's right," came a muffled voice from the pack on Carson's knees. He unfastened the zip and Vanta hopped half out, back to her normal shape. It was the first time she'd spoken since the race. "Two vehicles have been behind us since we left."

Carson shrugged. "Why would anybody follow us?"

"Well. . ." Eddie hesitated and gave another glance out of the back window. A pair of vans were just two cars behind. They changed lanes in unison as he watched. "While you were racing, something very strange happened."

Eddie quickly told them of his misadventure. Carson and Trix listened with increasing disbelief, then fear as they recalled how the AirBlitz team were dragged from the paddock.

"You're telling me they weren't officials?" said Carson as he picked out the pursuing vans.

Eddie shook his head. "They were posing as officials, but they kept calling themselves *agents*." He looked accusingly at Vanta. "No prizes for guessing what they're looking for."

If it were possible, Vanta's camera seemed to grow larger, giving them puppy eyes as she looked between them.

"OK, yes. They're looking for me. I . . . I ran away."

"From who?" asked Carson, although deep down he knew.

"From very bad people." Vanta zipped out of the pack and hovered in front of them, but out of view of the driver. "There's an eighty-seven per cent probability they're the same people who broke into your house."

Carson felt his blood run cold. "So they know I have you?"

"If they knew for sure, then they would have made a move much earlier." Vanta fluttered nervously. "They must have been watching all the games across the country, just in case."

"Is this why you changed shape earlier?" Eddie asked. "So they wouldn't recognize you?"

"Yes. I didn't think it was a great idea for the press to get detailed pictures."

"But can't they track you?" Trix asked with concern.

Vanta turned to look at her. "Only within close proximity, like inside the arena, can they detect my frequencies. When you connect me to the controller it helps mute those signals. And they don't know which drone I am." She swivelled to look at the three of them in turn. "Because I'm in disguise even now," she added quietly.

Carson nodded slowly. "When they came to my house..."

"They broke in on all the competitors," said Eddie, whose gaze hadn't left the vans. "Remember the crime wave reports? And that Agent Bevan admitted it was them."

Carson unclipped his seat belt and balanced on his knees, sitting backwards on his seat so he could watch the vans. "Why are they following us now?"

"Eddie's trick using AirBlitz for cover was brilliant, but it wouldn't have taken them long to realize their drone was nothing special," said Vanta as she joined him peering through the window. "And this close..."

"They can detect you," said Trix finishing the drone's sentence.

Carson tightly gripped the back of the seat. "Surely they won't try anything in the middle of London?"

Eddie shivered. "You didn't see what they were like back there. I reckon they don't want us setting foot on that train."

"We have to shake them off," said Vanta. "Leave that to me."

Vanta gave a little shiver. Then Carson saw the driver's satnav suddenly change route. Without giving it a second thought, the driver followed the map and pulled off the busy road.

Carson was impressed. "You hacked into the satnav. But weren't we safer surrounded by traffic?"

As if on cue, the pursuing vans followed and accelerated forward, splitting either side of their minivan. Eddie's eyes widened when he saw Agent Anders was at the wheel of one, Agent Bevan in the passenger seat. The other van contained a pair of almost identical goons who looked too big to fit inside. Their own driver glanced around in irritation as he suddenly noticed the danger.

"What the—?!"

His side window suddenly shattered as one of the thugs fired a Taser at him. The two metal darts hit the driver in the arm, then deployed a powerful electrical shock.

The driver jerked in his seat, dribbling and gurgling incoherently. His hands waved in the air as he let go of the steering wheel. Ordinarily the people carrier would have careened from the road – instead it veered into one van and bounced off, hitting the other. Having disconnected their seat belts earlier, Carson and Eddie were thrown from one side to the other with the two sharp impacts. But being caught between the vans meant their vehicle remained heading straight forward. . .

Straight towards a sharp bend in the road, marked by barrier of jagged black-and-white arrows.

Carson lunged for the steering wheel, but the heavy driver was slouched against it.

"We need to turn!" shouted Trix.

"I can't move him!"

"You can't drive, either!" shouted Eddie in panic.

"I can!" Vanta darted to the front and perched on the dashboard. She gave a slight wiggle which Carson now recognized as her "hacker face" and suddenly the van's dashboard lit up with the message: HANDS-FREE DRIVE ENGAGED. "Hold on!"

Controlling the people carrier remotely, Vanta slammed on the brakes. The screech and scent of burning rubber filled the van. Carson and Eddie were hurled forward, crashing into the seats in front. Trix was saved by her seat belt, but the breath was knocked from her. The menacing vans overshot them and hit their brakes too as the three vehicles took the sharp turn ahead.

Agent Anders wrestled the steering wheel as

her van hit the barrier in a shower of sparks. Vanta was driving too fast as she made the turn. The wheels on one side lifted from the ground. The little drone managed to hover in place as the car rolled – tumbling Carson, Trix and Eddie over one another as they rolled against the sliding door.

"Seat belts!" Vanta screeched. "You should have your seat belts on all the time!"

The top of their vehicle clipped Agent Anders's sparking van, pushing them back on to four wheels with a heavy jolt. Inside, the passengers rolled back to the floor in a chorus of screams. Trix and Eddie dropped themselves back into their seats and Carson found himself sitting in the front passenger seat as the unconscious man lolled against him.

"You are a terrible driver!" Eddie snapped at Vanta.

"I am more of a flyer... Hold on!" Vanta said as the electric engine gave a low whine and bolted ahead.

There were a couple of metallic clicks as the boys latched their seat belts. A quick check in the damaged rear-view mirror showed Carson that their pursuers were slowly catching up.

"We have to do something," he wailed desperately.

The dual carriageway ahead was peppered with cars, which Vanta slalomed through, accelerating up to eighty miles per hour. Several times Trix closed her eyes, convinced they were going to crash.

"I'll call the police!" Eddie's nerves were jangling as he fished his phone from his pocket.

"You could," said Vanta, "but they will hand me over."

Carson hadn't thought about that. He caught Trix's wide eyes. She gave a slight shake of her head.

Even Eddie didn't appear to like that idea. "Then we're going to have to give them the slip," he said firmly.

Vanta brightened. "OK. Then sit back and relax. Remember, I'm remotely piloting the van." Carson felt worried with the idea that a drone was going to be controlling *him*. "I'll be right back."

"Wait – what?"

Vanta flew straight through the broken passenger window and arced towards the van, drawing up to their right-hand side as the traffic ahead thinned out. Locked in positions by their seat belts, they could only watch in horror as the side door of the approaching van slid open, revealing the grinning goon who had fired the Taser. He had a bigger one in his hand, so big that he hefted it on to his shoulder like a rocket launcher.

"He's going to blow us up!" screeched Eddie.

Trix's fingers dug into her seat out of sheer fright. "I don't think so. I think he's going to taser the electric engine! We roll to a halt, then they've got us!"

The man took aim at the side of the boot, where the battery packs were stored. His finger flicked aside a safety guard across the trigger. There was nothing they could do to stop him.

At the same time Carson caught sight of what lay ahead – a set of traffic lights were on red and huge lorries were cutting across their path. If Vanta didn't stop them now then it didn't matter if the man fired or not.

In anticipation of a pending crash, Carson pushed himself back into his chair. His arms were shaking from the very effort. His attention was drawn back to the van as he caught movement behind it.

It was Vanta swooping down faster than he had ever seen her fly. A quick glance at the speedometer showed they had slowed to fifty miles per hour – but the world around them still whipped by in a blur.

They all watched the little drone disappear between the van's rear wheels and feared she would be crushed to oblivion.

There was a series of sharp electrical flashes from under the vehicle, similar to what Carson had witnessed during the first race when Vanta mysteriously took out their buzz-saw rival. It provided enough illumination for Carson to see the drone barely skimming over the tarmac was now growing.

Vanta was growing.

From a drone he could hold in his hand, he watched in astonishment as ribbons of electricity coursed along Vanta's fuselage as she expanded. He couldn't see any expansion joints in Vanta's fuselage; instead the drone's skin and chassis seemed to stretch until she was the size of a car. It all happened in seconds. In doing so she lifted the minivan up off the road, her suddenly enormous engines revving at maximum power.

The vehicle's rear wheels spun with a shrill shriek now they were no longer in contact with the road.

The goon dropped his weapon and clung to the doorframe for his life.

With open mouths, the children watched as Vanta rose above them. Then, with a sharp wiggle, she pitched the van off her. It tumbled through the air – smashing down on its roof in a cloud of metal fragments. It rolled half a dozen more times before slamming into a barrier. Miraculously, the two men inside dragged themselves clear of the wreckage as it caught fire. Carson finally remembered to look ahead.

The lights were still on red. The lorries still cutting across their path. And they hadn't slowed down.

"Red light! Red light!" he screamed, hoping Vanta could hear but it seemed she couldn't. They were at the point of no return – it would be impossible to even skid to a halt. Carson threw his arms over his head and braced for impact.

He didn't see Vanta had lined their minivan up at the perfect speed. They shot through the red light and a gap between two mighty juggernauts – with just centimetres to spare! The sound of truck horns blaring almost deafened them.

When Carson peeked again, the road ahead was empty. There was no sign of Agent Anders behind them. Vanta, now back to her normal size, soared through the smashed window and dropped on to the dashboard, doing a good impression of being exhausted.

"I need power," she gasped.

"Got it." Trix unfastened her seat belt and rummaged around in the glovebox, where she found the driver's phone charger. Snatching her bag from where it had tumbled, she extracted her toolkit.

"We're going to be late for our train," Eddie said, looking at his watch.

"We can't catch the train; that's the first place they'll look." Vanta flew on to the driver's head. "I'll drive us home. But first we need to do something about this guy."

Chapter 21
HOMEBOUND

Remotely controlling the people carrier, Vanta soon had them on the motorway and heading home. She sat on the dashboard, minimizing movement as she recharged from the phone charger Trix had rewired.

"Oh, nuts! My sister!" Eddie exclaimed. In all the excitement they had clean forgotten that she was supposed to meet them at the train station. "I'll message her. At least she can't shout."

He quickly typed that they were stuck in a horrendous traffic jam and wouldn't make the train, followed by a smiley face and, by accident, a fish.

WHAT?????? came the swift reply.

"Six question marks," he noted. "I don't think she's happy."

"Tell her we're getting a ride home from the organizers," Trix suggested.

Eddie dutifully typed the message and didn't have to wait long for the reply.

PICK ME UP RIGHT NOW!

He sighed. "All caps. It's almost like I can hear her voice. *Pick me up,*" he mimicked in a stroppy voice. He spoke aloud as he typed: "Can't. Car full. Don't worry. Race you home. XOX." Then after thinking about it he deleted the XOX. "Nah, she'd know something was seriously up if I put that."

Her reply came few seconds later: *OK. On train. Be careful. K*

"Ooh, she found the caps lock," said Eddie, showing them the message.

"It's cool having a name you can still spell with one letter," Trix noted with a faint smile.

Eddie nodded and, for the first time he could remember, he began to wonder if she wasn't as bad as he'd always assumed.

The poor driver remained out cold for another

fifteen minutes before the drone detected signs that he would soon be waking.

They pulled into the first service station they found to drop the driver off. It took all three of them to position him on a picnic bench in the darkest corner of the car park.

"Hurry," said Vanta. "He's showing signs of waking up."

"If we get caught doing this. . ." Eddie began.

"Shut up," Trix snapped at him. "Would you rather explain to him what we did to his van and why it's being driven by a drone?"

They made sure the driver was comfortable, then hopped straight back into the van and continued onwards.

Carson was on edge that their vehicle, with its shattered window, dents and scratches down one side and a broken headlight would attract police attention. Surprisingly it didn't, thanks to Vanta carefully monitoring the traffic ahead. She perched on the dashboard, silently recharging using the cables Trix had rewired.

For the next hour they sat in silence; Vanta had claimed that she needed to dedicate all the energy she had left to driving, not talking. Carson thought it was just an excuse not to answer their growing list of questions.

Eddie was snoring loudly, a stream of dribble working its way down his chin and on to the window his head was resting against, when Vanta finally stirred back to life.

"We'll be home in forty minutes," she said.

"And what's to stop the bad guys from finding us there?" The question had been weighing heavily on Trix.

Eddie pulled a face and extended his arms, as if to say *I'm the man!* "You both think I do nothing, but as manager my job is to look ahead. Remember when I registered us with the league I gave false names, addresses, phone numbers." Eddie tapped the side of his head to indicate how smart he was. "I didn't want us to get caught and me get grounded for life by my parents. To Marcus Nation we're just three kids. And if anybody asks you're Carson McFartson –" he ignored Carson's scowl "– you're Trix Fontana and I'm Eddie McSmooth."

Trix extended her fist and looked him straight in the eye. "I don't give compliments easily, Eddie.

But you're a devious genius." With a grin, Eddie fist-bumped her.

"But they came in my house, remember," Carson pointed out.

"Don't worry about that," Vanta assured him. "It was too dark, so they didn't have a chance to identify you or me. The only thing they do know is we're the Carsonators who won the regional heat, and they still don't know that was me. Besides, it's a big region. They didn't enter Eddie or Trix's homes—"

"They broke into other racer's homes," Eddie pointed out.

"But you were smart enough not to use your real details."

Eddie beamed with delight. "Yeah, I was, wasn't I." He ignored Trix's overly loud tut.

"So I suspect they were searching every house, trying to pinpoint my weak frequency signature in the neighbourhood. You have to remember that I am very . . . secret technology. They can't afford to turn up in force and attract the attention of news reporters."

Trix snapped her fingers. "That's why they were searching the warehouse! Remember that van? I bet that was them."

Carson felt himself relax a little and leaned back in his seat. "So, my first question is, who are they, exactly?"

Vanta paused as she shuffled on the dashboard so she could face them. "A secret government department. And no, not your government. They're obviously working under the radar, or we'd be in much bigger trouble."

"Did they make you?" asked Trix.

"I escaped from a special testing facility."

Trix threw her hands up in despair. "Great! Eddie was right. You really are a killer robot!"

Vanta's single camera eye twirled around, somehow managing to make her look sad. "Not at all. My father created me as a weapon to defend people, not for war." Her voice lifted with a trace of pride. "I was to soar the skies, protecting civilians. Preventing crimes . . . making the world a safer place."

Trix leaned forward in her seat. "And then you short-circuited?"

"No. Then I learned that the military were very impressed. But they didn't see me as a peacekeeper. They saw me as a weapon. My father refused to help them with that, but he had little choice. My fate was to be sent to the battlefield. Sent to kill."

Carson felt a shiver run through him at the very thought.

Vanta hovered so she could see them all. "I didn't want to do that, so I escaped and went on the run for days." She dropped back down on the dash and focused on driving. "I was always able to keep one step ahead but despite everything I did, they were still able to track me. I mean, it's not like I'm an everyday drone, so I do stand out." She fluttered her front rotors, one then the other, reminding Carson of the way a weightlifter might flex his arms. He smiled as she continued. "But my power was fading and it wasn't long before I was approaching emergency shutdown. I spotted a scrapyard; it had a few aircraft parts in there, and I thought it was someplace I could at least hide in. Once my batteries are completely depleted, well, that would be the end for me."

Trix was thoughtful. "You just vanished off their radar."

Vanta wiggled as she nodded. "Yes. They had an approximate location, but nothing accurate. I'm afraid entering that first race was a mistake. They must have had people there just in case."

Carson rubbed the scar on the back of his head. "And this little racer is your disguise. When I found you I really wasn't imagining things. You grew in size and lifted me out."

"Yes, using my tow cable."

"So you could have run out of power lifting me out? You could have died?"

"It was my final gamble. We both could have died down there. I couldn't let that happen."

Carson was touched by the gesture. He held out his hand and Vanta hopped on to his palm. He looked closely at her, trying to find any joins or gaps that indicated she could grow. "How do you do it?"

Vanta laughed. "Even I don't know that, and I'm really smart. My father constructed me from a new super-polymer based on something called graphene. All I know is that it takes a lot of power to swap sizes."

"If the military wanted to send you into a battle zone," Trix said thoughtfully, "does that mean you're armed?"

Vanta cagily bobbed side to side. "Mmm ... but I only use boppers as a last resort."

"Boppers?" spluttered Eddie. "What kind of weapon is that?"

Vanta ignored him. "It's always better to out-think an opponent. I didn't ever want to use them. That's why I ran away in the first place." She paused. "There's not that much juice spare in this vehicle. I'm going to have to focus on the drive."

As she lapsed into silence, the three friends settled down, somehow feeling safer knowing the truth behind the drone. Vanta had proved her worth against the agents, and they felt safe in the knowledge she was there to watch over them. Eddie even managed to fall asleep on the final leg home, with Trix following moments later.

After a half hour, a question that had been bugging Carson returned.

"You wouldn't happen to know anything about mysterious train tickets and a hotel suite, would you?"

"Why would I?"

"Because I saw how you hacked into the satnav, and Marcus Nation looked very confused when I thanked him."

There was a long, telling pause.

"I knew how important it was for you to be there."

The little drone sounded almost apologetic.

Carson tried not to laugh. "I think that was the nicest thing anybody has ever done for me. Although maybe I shouldn't ask how you paid for it."

It was the dead of night when they all returned home. Eddie and Trix were able to sneak inside without any trouble, while Carson didn't even attempt to keep silent as he turned the key in the door. A quick check around revealed that his dad wasn't even home.

After she was plugged in, Vanta said she would remotely dispose of their vehicle, but Carson suggested returning it back to where they had left the driver. Vanta dutifully set about her task while Carson fought to stay awake, a job he was very unsuccessful at. . .

Chapter 22
TEAM DECISIONS

The next few days unfolded without any further incidents, and they stopped racing with Vanta in an attempt to keep a low profile. Carson was worried about leaving the drone alone in the house, so he took her everywhere in his backpack, connecting her to his controller to help disrupt her telltale frequencies.

Eddie confirmed that the ten-thousand-pound prize money had been paid into a bank account Vanta had set up online. The credit card arrived a few days later in the post, dutifully delivered to a PO box Vanta had set up to avoid using any of their home addresses.

Running to a cash machine, they drew out enough to pay Kay to keep quiet, and Trix claimed back all the money she had previously spent on the Carsonators. Even so, that had barely dented the account. They agreed to be sensible and not touch too much of it. The last thing they wanted was to draw attention.

However, that plan crumbled when they decided to visit the shopping centre for "a bit of equipment". The lure of polished marble, sparking glass and bright lights was too much: new trainers silently screamed to Carson to be bought. Their jeans suddenly seemed too worn out and in dire need of replacement.

Eddie pressed himself against a shop window. "Wow, I need to have that jacket." he exclaimed, despite never having any interest in fashion previously. "You know, for the team image!"

In they went. Out they came laden with shopping bags filled with things they'd never been able to afford before, all in the name of "team image". Then it was Trix's turn as an invisible force drew her to the phone shop and the gleaming mobile slowly rotating in a display cabinet.

"That is a serious piece of hardware!" She could even hear a heavenly choir, although Eddie pointed out that was just the shop music playing. That didn't prevent them all walking out with top-of-the-line models.

"So we can talk to each other *properly*," justified Trix.

"Not like on those *old* phones," agreed Eddie.

Exhausted from their very responsible spending of funds, they celebrated their national victory over an enormous pizza in the food court.

With a mouthful of pepperoni and cheese crust, Eddie excitedly played with his new phone. The screen was already covered in thick, greasy fingerprints, but underneath them a notification dinged: an email about their trip to Seoul had just come through.

"The hotel and plane tickets are being arranged, they just need me to email copies of our passports." He punched the air with his fist. "We're going to South Korea!"

Trix drummed the table excitedly. "Here's to us winners!"

It was left to Carson to bring the jubilant mood

crashing down. "We can't go."

Eddie threw a cheesy chunk of pizza at Carson's forehead, leaving a string of cheddar. "Are you serious? We're the UK champs. This is the world championship, it's our *duty* to be there. We have *the* best drone in the universe. They're paying to fly us over there. And there is a *fifty-thousand-quid* prize. It's a no-brainer!"

"We'd be walking straight into a trap, especially if you want to email our passports, with our real names? Don't you think those agents will be waiting for us? They might not know who we are right now, but the moment we roll up there. . ." He shook his head at the frightening thought.

Truth be told, Carson had been worried that things had been so quiet. It was obvious the Carsonators were from the region – their pictures were out there, plastered all over drone racing sites – yet no shadowy agents had turned up. But he couldn't shake the feeling they were out there, watching. Waiting.

Eddie's appetite vanished and he put his wedge down without a bite taken.

Carson avoided looking at them. "If we get

caught, we lose Vanta. Why take the risk?"

"We only have her because of the race," said Eddie with a hint of betrayal. "She wants to do it, or she could fly off any time. We want to do it. So what's your problem?"

Trix pouted and thrust herself back in her chair, arms folded and a scowl on her face. "I think his problem is about the fact it was me who flew us over the finishing line and not him."

"What?" Carson had no idea where this was coming from.

"You've been weird with me ever since we won."

"I've been weird with you because we had *a secret government agency chasing us*!"

Eddie poked his thumb against his chest. "I was the one they beat up!"

"They didn't actually hurt you. They made you sit in a chair," Carson pointed out.

Eddie ignored him, continuing: "*And* I was the one who bravely didn't give anything away! And I still want us to go and race." He angrily stabbed for forefinger towards Carson. "You're just being selfish!"

"I'm being realistic!" Carson glanced as his pack lying on the table. Vanta was nestled inside and being quiet. He wished she'd speak up to defend him.

Eddie pushed his glasses up as they tried to slide from his nose and lowered his voice to try and assure Carson. "If they knew who we were then they would have turned up already."

"That's my point. If we don't make any mistakes they won't find us here. We're safe. If we go to the finals, all they have to do is wait for us to turn up."

"We have Vanta with us," said Trix desperately. "We'd be safe, in a foreign country! And we've been a step ahead all the time."

"I can't lose her..." Carson's voice was barely audible.

Eddie stood and snatched up his bags. He refused to meet Carson's eyes. "Typical. The moment we start getting somewhere, it all falls apart. Thanks for nothing."

"You're supposed to be our manager. Shouldn't you be worried about the risks?" huffed Carson.

"I got a taste of winning," Eddie snapped back as he haughtily walked away without bothering to look back. Carson stared at the remains of the pizza, his own appetite gone. He heard Trix drag her chair back and stand. She picked up her shopping, slowly looping each bag over her shoulder.

"You might not like the way we won the last race, but you were right when you said that we won it as team. We should complete this, even if we lose, because the three of us are better together than alone."

"It's not about the race..." mumbled Carson, although part of him wondered if she had a point. The last few days they had all been on edge and hadn't dared take Vanta out for a race. However, the little drone had been restless and desperate to take to the air.

Every night, Carson expected the house to be raided by sinister government agents ... but they didn't come. Instead he and Vanta had fallen into a routine of her reading stories aloud as he drifted to sleep.

Trix took her last bag and looked sadly at him. "If we're not a team, Carson, what are we?"

Carson's mouth hung open in an unspoken answer. Trix shook her head. Then she walked away.

Carson snatched his half-filled Coke and noisily slurped from it, hoping the noise would drown out his own thoughts.

Vanta's muffled voice came from his bag. "Why are they going?"

"Because they're idiots."

How could such an amazingly fun day have suddenly turned so dismal? *They're just greedy*, Carson tried to convince himself. They had planned to go bowling and maybe even to the cinema, but that was clearly not happening. The Coke tasted flat, so he put the plastic cup down with a hollow thud that got disapproving looks from the family at the table next to him.

With a sigh, he slung his backpack over one shoulder and gathered his shopping. "Come on, let's go home."

"Maybe you should go after them and say sorry?"

"Are you crazy? I'm not apologizing!" Carson snapped so loud he got puzzled looks from passers-by. One lady even squeezed the hand of her young daughter and pulled her away from the glowering boy who was arguing with himself.

Carson walked from the food court, back into the main avenue of designer shops. He glanced around the artfully placed trees and barrow stalls selling handmade crafts, all under an enormous arched glass ceiling that trapped the summer sun like a greenhouse. There was no sign of Trix or Eddie. *Not that it matters*, he thought; he had nothing more to say to them.

He headed to the escalator leading down to the ground floor. He'd decided to go home, download a film and watch it with Vanta. He stepped on to the moving escalator just as he noticed who was standing on the upward side. It was Agent Anders, without her shades and dressed in a black bomber jacket and baseball cap, and black shirt – but he instantly recognized her from the minivan chase. And she was looking straight at him. Her wrist shot to her mouth as she urgently spoke into a microphone concealed there.

Carson pushed himself backwards – straight into an elderly woman stepping on to the escalator behind him who squealed as he shoved past her, ignoring her comment about the youth of today.

And he ran.

Chapter 23
TRAPPED!

Carson's new trainers squealed on the polished marble floor, making him instantly regret buying them; what had been wrong with the old ones? The long avenues of the shopping centre didn't have many places to hide, but he weaved between a pair of kiosks and across a footbridge connecting one side to the other.

On the level below, music suddenly struck up as the ornate fountain began to spit water droplets in formation as part of its hourly show. Surrounding shoppers stopped to watch, the crowds adding further cover for Carson.

Vanta's voice was barely audible from his bag. "I detected familiar biometrics."

"They've found us."

"Oh no. It must have been the credit card!"

"But they don't know who I am!"

"All they had to do was wait and track the prize money into the account, then wait for the credit card to be used. The moment you started spending cash today, they would have narrowed their search down to right here and then identified you from the league photos."

Now on the other side of the avenue, Carson crouched behind a potted plant twice his size and peeped across. He could see Anders running to a halt as she met up with Bevan, who was similarly dressed. They both straightened up and looked around like meerkats. Agent Anders was already on her mobile phone.

"Agent Bevan is here too."

"Let me see."

Carson ignored the odd looks people were giving him as he unzipped his pack and Vanta flew on to his shoulder. She gave a little hacker-face wiggle.

"What did you do?"

Vanta sounded proud of herself. "Accessed the shopping centre's security cameras and put them out of action. They won't be able to use them to track us!"

As if to confirm that, Anders angrily hung up her phone and started talking into her wrist.

"Who's she talking to...?" Carson asked nervously.

"There!" The sharp voice came from his left. Another two men, dressed identically – apparently all in black was a government agent's idea of inconspicuous – were sprinting towards him.

Carson sprang into a run, shoving through the thickening crowds now also gathering on the balconies to watch the fountain display below. Using her rotors to balance herself, Vanta stayed on his shoulder and Carson had the momentary image that he must look like a twenty-first-century pirate.

Another pair of agents suddenly loomed ahead of him. They had already begun to slow down, knowing they had him. Carson stopped. He was trapped.

"Get ready to run!" Vanta shuddered a little – then the fire alarm howled throughout the building.

As usual when an alarm sounded, nobody moved, other than to peer around wondering if it was a deadly fire or merely a drill. The agents hesitated too.

Then the sprinklers activated. Hundreds of them, mounted on the curved glass roof, unleashed a torrent of cold rain. A chorus of screams arose from people who were suddenly darting for cover. In an instant people flowed between Carson and the agents.

The agents, realizing they were about to lose their prey, shoved their way through the throng – but Carson was already running for the bridge. It wasn't the best option, as it led back to Anders and Bevan, but he had no choice.

He felt a firm hand on his arm as one of the agents caught up. Vanta leapt from his shoulder and banked into the hand. The agent shrieked in pain and immediately let go as the drone's propellers, grazing his knuckles with the horrid sound of a paper shredder.

The man sucked his fingers – and didn't see Carson arcing his shopping bag around like an Olympian hammer thrower. Packed with various heavy boxes, slammed straight into the agent's face. The bag's straps broke, pitching the boxes over the edge of the bridge, where they smashed apart on the stone floor below. The agent staggered, his feet slipping in the wet floor, and he crashed on to his back, whimpering in his own silent world of pain.

The other three agents behind him stopped and simply blocked Carson's escape. Anders and Bevan confidently walked towards him from the other side of the bridge.

"We don't want to hurt you," Anders cautioned, while at the same time drawing a gun. Carson spotted the black and yellow stripes on it, and recognized it as a Taser like the one that knocked out their driver. "We just want the drone."

"You can't have her!" Carson's damp hair clung to his forehead, sending rivulets of rain into his eyes.

"It doesn't belong to you, Carson."

Well, now she knew his name.

"She doesn't belong to you either, Agent Anders," he said.

Anders looked as if her patience was about to snap. She raised the Taser in a threatening manner. "It's not a *she*, kid. It's an it. A piece of military hardware that isn't safe amongst the general population."

Carson glanced behind. The three agents stood stock-still in the deluge. Peering over the balcony, he was now directly over the ornate fountain, which was still playing its jaunty tune.

He was trapped and Agent Anders knew it.

"The way I see it is, you give it up right now and things don't have to get messy. Or, we shoot you and take it anyway." She smiled. "The choice is yours."

Carson's fists bunched. If they were going to take Vanta by force, then he'd at least give them a fight.

"Do you trust me?" whispered Vanta. Carson gave a single subtle nod. "When I say jump, don't hesitate."

Carson's heart pounded in his chest and he nodded again.

Vanta lifted into the air. "I'll come quietly, Agent Anders. Just put the Taser down – you're scaring the boy."

Anders paused . . . then slid the Taser back into the holster under her jacket. Vanta turned to Carson.

"Thank you for trying to help me, and I'm sorry things didn't work out the way you wanted." She slowly drifted forward and out over the drop. "So now I only have one thing left to say . . . JUMP!"

Carson didn't hesitate – nor did he fully know what Vanta intended. He gripped the metal barrier on the bridge and vaulted over it, plunging towards the stone floor far below. . .

Chapter 24
RUNAWAY

Carson's stomach suddenly filled with butterflies as he plummeted towards the ground with arms and legs spinning like windmills in a storm.

He heard Agent Anders scream something and saw Vanta dive towards him. Electrical surges crackled over her body and, in the blink of an eye, she expanded to the size of his bed. She caught him on his back, mid-fall. The impact knocked the breath from him and he felt her wobble.

"OOF! You're heavier than you look. Hold on!"

Carson threw his arms either side of Vanta as she sharply banked upwards. The acceleration was so savage that Carson felt his grip slip and his cheeks pull backwards. The sprinkler rain now felt as if he was being pelted by stones as they shot towards the roof.

"Vanta!" Carson yelled, seconds away from impact with the glass roof.

The concealed compartment in Vanta's belly popped open and, with a loud bang, a missile shot towards the glass roof and detonated!

Glass exploded and the metal spars holding it all in place were torn away as Vanta zoomed through the newly created opening, and out into the rain-free blue summer sky.

Carson howled in victory, twisting so he could see the shopping centre recede far below them. The wind stung his face, but he didn't care.

He was flying.

He was really flying.

Luckily, Carson didn't live too far from the shopping centre; at least, not if you were travelling well above roads. Vanta aimed straight for his house, and they soon landed in the back garden. Carson saw the twitch of a curtain as a nosy neighbour peered out.

The instant they touched down, Vanta shrank back to her miniature form. She hovered uncertainly in the air, her voice sounding weak. "Get what you need, then we must go. They will be heading straight here."

As usual, his dad wasn't home, so Carson snatched a towel to dry his hair and changed into fresh clothes. He stuffed a few clean tops and underwear into his backpack.

The sound of an over-revving engine outside caught his attention. Five black SUVs were speeding down the road towards his house. If that wasn't alarming enough, he saw his dad's car approach from the other end of the street.

He hurried his packing, throwing in his toothbrush, a packet of Penguin biscuits and, on impulse, his passport. All done, he looked back out to see the vehicles had stopped right outside and filled the road with stern, black-suited agents armed with a variety of electronic detectors they waved in the air, searching for telltale signals from Vanta. He saw his dad begin a heated conversation with Anders.

"Dad..." Carson uttered under his breath. He

saw the concern on his father's face as his father found his house key and slowly walked to the front door. He was obviously cooperating with the agents; Carson could only imagine what he had been told.

With time running out, he and Vanta darted out the back door and clambered over the neighbour's fence at the back of the garden. As they made it on to the street, he shoved his clothes tightly in his pack to make room for Vanta and she dropped inside.

Carson glanced up as the sound of helicopters grew and he pressed himself against the wall as two black aircraft rushed overhead. Without looking back, he sprinted to the end of the road, putting his house as far behind him as possible and leaving him wondering if he'd ever see home again . . . or his dad.

Considering it had been such a lovely, warm summer day, Carson couldn't quite believe how cold it was at night. He pulled his coat tighter around him, but it only served to make him shiver more.

Wandering the streets had proved increasingly perilous as additional black SUVs drove quickly past in convoy, forcing him to duck down alleys and hide behinds rubbish skips. At one point he counted six helicopters crisscrossing the sky at low altitude, obviously searching for them.

Vanta had put herself into sleep mode in case she accidentally emitted any telltale signals they could use to track her down – just in time, as a large military truck growled past with a spinning radar dish on the roof.

If Carson had had any questions about the serious trouble they were in, the scale of the search closing in on them left him with no doubt.

He briefly considered visiting Eddie or Trix, but thought they wouldn't be pleased to see him, especially if he was being followed by the country's entire military ... and he couldn't be sure if they were safe either. He felt powerless. Before powering down, Vanta had instructed him not to phone or text anybody, as the agents would be able to trace the call back to his phone and find him. His new phone remained switched off.

Night started to fall and with it came rain. Carson hid out in the old derelict cinema complex on the edge of town. With part of the roof intact, at least it was dry, and the old wooden seats may have been musty, but they provided something to sit on.

It had once been a grand theatre, and the beautifully crafted walls and ceiling were now weathered away to nothing more than warped wood.

Carson poked around the lobby, complete with smelly water-stained carpet and old decaying popcorn counters. There was a sad atmosphere common to places that were once filled with happy people. He began to wonder if his parents had come here when they were younger.

That thought was replaced by a more chilling one when he discovered the electricity was disconnected; would Vanta have enough power left to wake up? He kicked the rotting countertop apart into small planks and hurried into the main theatre. He built a small pyre on the concrete floor in the space where the screen once stood. As he did, he anxiously watched as Vanta powered back up. It seemed to take an awfully long time before Carson heard the reassuring BEE-BOP. The drone ignited the pyre by producing sparks from a pair of wires Carson carefully attached to her power orb.

The fire still didn't stop Carson from shivering, but it kept the darkness at bay. Vanta sat on an old seat but didn't say much more. He suspected that the transformation and effort in carrying him had severely depleted her batteries, but she didn't complain. The problem was, he had no way of recharging her.

He glanced at the dancing shadows around them. He was filled with dread about Vanta completely draining her batteries. The idea that the agents could take her from him was bad enough, but losing her for ever. . . How could he handle another loss like that? But then again, he couldn't stay on the run for much longer.

He replayed the last week through his mind.

"You said you were created by your father," he said, poking the fire to invigorate it.

"Of course. He made me. He's my father."

"What's his name?"

"Professor Jira Zushi. He's such an amazingly clever man. He told me he had dreams of changing the world, stopping wars, ending crime . . . and he said it would start with me. That's why he made me intelligent and gave me emotions. He thought it would make all the difference in the world. But the military didn't agree with him."

"Do you miss him?"

Vanta was thoughtful for a moment. "Yes. When I was alone in the scrapyard I thought I would never see him again. Never see anybody again. It made me very sad. Then you came along."

Carson smiled as he held his hands to the fire to warm his fingers. Then something she said came back to him. "When you said the military didn't agree, you mean about giving you a personality?"

"They didn't want a weapon that worried about hurting people. They liked everything else about the technology my father invented, but they intended to wipe my neural network."

"That sounds awful."

"Oh, I would still be smart, but without emotions. Like your phone. I mean, right now your phone isn't at all worried about you shivering. It isn't concerned that you're going to catch a cold out here."

Carson burst into laughter and fed more pieces of broken wood into the fire to keep it going. He watched a fountain of embers dance into the air. "You sound like my mum," he said wistfully.

"Do you miss her?"

Now it was Carson's turn to pause. He gave a sharp breath to stop himself from welling up as he always did when he thought of her.

"Every single day. She died of. . ." The words stuck in his throat.

"I know," said Vanta softly. Carson looked questioningly at her. "You forget I can access all sorts of records." With a little buzz from her engines, Vanta hopped on to his knee to get a better look at him. "You don't have to talk about her if you don't want to."

"I worry if I don't talk about her, I'll forget her. Like Dad has."

"Your dad hasn't forgotten about her."

Carson gave a disbelieving sniff. "Now I know you're making that up. He's never home. He doesn't care. . ." His chest heaved as he fought back the tears that threatened to spill. He had never been able to open up to his friends, and now he couldn't stop talking. "I think he'd be happier if I wasn't around either. Then he could start again. . ." He rubbed his eyes, feeling suddenly embarrassed for the outburst.

"You really don't know, do you?"

Carson felt a knot form in his stomach. "Know what?"

"Your dad nearly lost the house you're living in.

He used every penny he had to take care of your mother. He's currently working three different jobs to keep the house and to feed you, to keep you from having to go through any more changes. The doctors have warned him to take it easy, in case he exhausts himself too much. He's doing all of that because he loves you, Carson. You're all he has left."

He wanted to believe it, but instead he just felt angry. "That's rubbish! How could you know that?"

"I accessed his bank account and medical records. It wasn't hard to piece the truth together."

"I don't believe it."

"All you have to do is ask him."

Carson wiped away the tears using his sleeve. Now something else was bothering him. "I should have warned him not to go home. They've probably thrown him in a cell. Asking him questions about you. . ." He stared guiltily at his feet. "Maybe I should have told him?" he whispered almost to himself.

Vanta nervously shuffled on his knee. "This has gone too far. I've put you all in danger. That's why I'm going to turn myself in."

"No."

"Unlike your toaster, I care about you, Carson.

You can't live a life on the run because of me."

"They'll erase you!"

"That's the way it must be."

Again, tears welled in the corners of Carson's eyes. "I don't want that. You're all I have left. I don't want you to go!"

"And I don't want you to suffer."

Carson's throat was dry. He shook his head, refusing to accept what she said. Vanta alighted back on the oil drum and Carson stood, anxiously shifting from one foot to the other, but with nowhere to go.

"But before I go, there is one thing I want to do." She hovered in front of him. "I want to race, one last time."

"You want to *what*?" Carson didn't understand.

"When we flew from the shopping centre this evening, your heart rate was elevated, and adrenaline was pumping through your body. You felt good, right?"

Carson couldn't deny it. Clinging to Vanta and soaring over the rooftops . . . that had been magical.

"And that's how I feel when I race," Vanta said, performing a little figure of eight in the air. "It feels like *that's* what I was built for."

Now he understood. "You want to go to Seoul? And you want to win."

"The prize money would save your father. He wouldn't have to work himself to death. . . You could both start living properly again."

"Ha!" Carson kicked a can into the darkness. "Great. Well, in case you forgot, I don't have a team any more. And there's no way I could convince them to give me all the prize money."

"Well, if you ask nicely. . ." came a voice from the shadows.

Carson spun around as Eddie and Trix stepped from the shadows. He couldn't hide the relief he felt. "You're OK! What are you doing here?"

Trix had her phone in her hand. "We received anonymous messages about what had happened."

"Can't they track that?" Carson looked at Vanta, who managed to angle her blades into a nonchalant shrug.

"I sent a heavily encrypted message that will take them weeks to work out."

Eddie continued. "So we managed to get out before the cavalry arrived."

"The cavalry are the good guys," Trix pointed out. "I hung back to spy on them. They didn't go in the house so they probably think we're still home."

"And I got Kay to cover for us again," Eddie added with a grin. He held out his fist to Carson. "So how about it? Shall the Carsonators fly one last time?"

Despite himself, Carson couldn't stop the smile pulling at his cheeks. He fist-bumped Eddie. They kept their knuckles pressed together as Trix joined in with a bump, the trio now locked together.

"Let's do this," Trix smiled. "Let's race!"

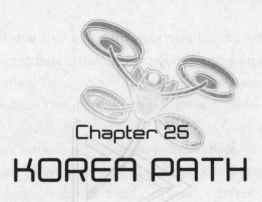

Chapter 25
KOREA PATH

The Carsonators were buzzing with so much nervous energy that they knew sleep was out of the question. Instead they used the time around the fire to charge Vanta as much as they could – Trix had thought to bring along a portable phone charger – and plan their trip to Seoul.

Trix was convinced that the last thing the government agents would expect was them to actually turn up to the world championship, but she was pretty sure they would be watching the airports just in case their tickets were used. That was no problem for Vanta, who, in just a few

minutes of shimmying with her hacker face –
which had everybody crying with laughter, as the
little drone looked as if she was wriggling her
bum – had booked them new flights under fake
names.

"We don't have passports in those names,"
Carson pointed out. Vanta assured him that she had
a plan, and the money to buy the tickets wouldn't be
easily traced back to their bank account. All they had
to do was turn up for their new flight.

However, there was a wrinkle which Vanta
couldn't help them with.

"We can't travel without an adult," Trix pointed
out. "At least somebody who can hand us over to
the airline. That's the law," she added knowingly,
although she didn't admit it was something she had
only seen on TV.

Everybody looked expectantly at Eddie. It took
him a moment to realize what the silent question
was.

"My sister? No way! She may technically be an
adult, but she won't help us again."

"She's not as bad as you think," Carson pointed
out. "And we'll give her more money."

"We're talking about several days and going halfway around the planet. She might be an idiot, but she's not stupid!"

Carson was watching Vanta closely. She was moving slowly and in small bursts, clearly on the last dregs of power. When Carson tried to ask her about it, she changed the subject. Vanta had sucked the phone charger's power dry in minutes, but Carson doubted it was enough.

He lowered his voice. "If we don't get her charged up very soon then we're going to lose her. I mean, for ever."

Eddie nodded solemnly and stared at his phone as he summoned the courage to call his sister. She answered on the first ring.

"Where the heck are you?" she hissed before he could say anything.

"I can't really tell you right now—"

"Tracy's parents have been calling and Carson's dad has been around asking if they know anything about you lot racing drones."

"What did you tell them?"

"What do you think? I lied."

"You are a brilliant, sis," he said, and he was

surprised to feel he meant it. "Carson's dad doesn't approve of him racing."

"But then these guys in black suits turned up and now everybody is going crazy wanting to know where you are!".

Eddie hesitated. "I need you to cover for us again."

Her voice rose in pitch so she was clearly heard by the others. "What?"

"We're going to Korea." There was silence from the other side of the line. "You still there?"

"You're in a world of trouble if you do."

"We already are. We have to go to the world championships. I don't have time to explain over the phone. . ."

Tell her we'll pay her if we win, Trix mouthed to him.

Eddie's brow furrowed as he moved away to continue the conversation in private.

Carson and Trix strained to listen, but couldn't hear anything except indistinct words. After almost a minute he returned, shoulders slumped and head bowed in defeat. Carson could already feel the bad news coming. If they couldn't board the aeroplane then their last adventure was over before it had even begun. Eddie stood close to the fire, warming his hands.

"So?" asked Trix impatiently.

"She said covering for us would be too risky." Silence fell across the group.

"Well, that's it, then," sighed Carson. "Thanks for trying."

"So I said we'd give her a thousand pounds," Eddie mumbled. He glanced at the others, who looked expectantly at him to continue. He sighed. "She said it wasn't enough."

"How much is enough?" snapped Trix.

"The thousand pounds ... and she wants to come with us." Eddie looked more wretched than before. "She said she's not going to refuse a free holiday and that the airline wouldn't let us onboard without an adult." He was surprised when Carson and Trix whooped with delight and fist-bumped one another.

"Brilliant!" yelled Carson. "Vanta, can you fix another ticket?"

"Already on it!"

Eddie watched in despair. "Kay's coming with us! Don't you see how bad that is?"

Clearly they didn't.

*

The next morning, they took a private car arranged by Vanta, who now didn't move and barely spoke in an effort to preserve power. They all agreed that the agents were probably keeping an eye on public transport, so they would have to be as covert as possible if they were to make it to the airport.

The car had first picked Kay up at the staff entrance of a restaurant in town. She had run through the busy restaurant in a flurry of apologies, convinced the agents were on her heels. The car had then driven to the cinema, and Kay had told the baffled driver to circle the building twice to check they weren't being followed. Only then did the others quickly bundle inside.

"The airport!" Carson urgently instructed the driver, then threw a pile of cash at him.

"Right away, sir!" snapped the driver, as he had quickly calculated the tip on his lap was four times the price of the trip.

In the car, Kay laid down her rules.

"OK. I have no intention of getting arrested or watching your stupid competition. I want to see Seoul; the city's supposed to be amazing." Her expression or tone never betrayed a moment of excitement as she added, "I suppose it's fun, running from secret government spies and being a rebel." Then she bowed her head so her hair covered her face and returned to messaging on her phone. Without looking up, she added, "And I want to sleep on the plane. Maybe watch a few movies. I don't want to have to talk to any of you."

"I can promise you that we all agree," said Eddie firmly. "And if I ever grow up to be like you, feel free to throw me out of a plane."

Kay looked sidelong at him. "If you get me arrested, you won't have to wait that long."

Checking in at the airport was surprisingly effortless, despite Carson, Trix and Eddie trying not to look guilty. Vanta's last trick was to hack into the airline's computer and momentarily change all the passenger names to match their passports. As soon as the tickets were printed, she swapped them back to the fake names. The military were undoubtedly monitoring passports, but the change was so swift it was unlikely to be noticed.

Three hours later they took off. Trix had used the time in the airport to plug Vanta into a power socket, and on board, Carson connected her to the aircraft's USB charger. It seemed to rouse the little drone back to life as he discreetly held her up so she could look out of the window.

"I've never been this high," she exclaimed. "Wow. It's so weird flying *inside* a plane!"

The three of them relaxed back in their seats. Vanta had made sure Kay had been upgraded to business class so she wasn't sitting with them. For once, Eddie didn't complain. He was quite happy for the peace and quiet.

While the others watched films and Vanta sat recharging on his tray table, Carson stared out of the window. He felt a twinge of guilt that he hadn't warned his dad, or somehow told him that they were headed halfway around the world. He hoped Vanta had been right about the prize money; maybe it would change things for them?

With regret, he realized he had talked more to Vanta in the last couple of weeks than to his dad in the last year. He spent another hour wrestling with what he would tell his father about his adventure.

Would he be furious? Would he understand? With no answer to the question, he eventually fell into a deep sleep as the aircraft powered its way into the night sky towards Asia...

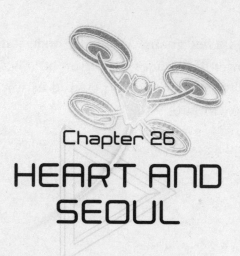

Chapter 26

HEART AND SEOUL

Arriving in Seoul was an assault on the senses. A Constructor League representative was waiting for them, holding up a CARSONATORS sign. They felt a moment of anxiety with their team name being so prominently displayed, just in case the agents had tracked them this far.

Eddie jabbed Carson in the ribs. "Told you it was a dumb name. Now everybody knows you're here."

The young Korean woman holding the sign breathlessly introduced herself, speaking with a slight American accent. She was more excited to see them than they were to be in Korea.

"My name is Hyo, and I will look after you while you are here. It's so exciting to meet you all!" Before they could reply she rapidly continued. "Yes, they've just walked out!"

Carson frowned. "Huh?"

"The car is waiting for us. Just push it sideways. And yes, make sure there's enough noodles."

"Either I am seriously jet-lagged, or her English is not as good as she thinks it is," Kay muttered to Carson.

Hyo led the way, still talking to herself. It wasn't until they were outside that Carson realized she was wearing a Bluetooth headset that covered one ear and was receiving a constant stream of requests, which meant every other sentence was directed at the voice on the other end.

Despite the sleep they had snatched on the flight, they were all quite tired as they drove into the city, which seemed to be built from countless skyscrapers, many lit up with neon strips as night began to fall. The Han River appeared to one side as they drove further into the sprawling metropolis and their guide, who seemed to know everything about the city, excitedly pointed out landmarks.

Hyo drew their attention to the Sangam Stadium, bathed in white lights that picked out its distinctive angular roof. "That is where the world championship will be held tomorrow," she said. "Everybody is super excited that you came! There was a lot of speculation that you wouldn't attend because you never confirmed your tickets and most competitors arrived yesterday. Many people still think you are not coming!"

"We like to maintain a sense of mystery," grinned Eddie. "It keeps our competitors on their toes."

They drove through wide boulevards packed with traffic across several lanes, with numerous side streets branching off in a riot of colourful signs luring visitors into shops. Hyo then began telling Kay about the best places to shop. Kay's eyes sparkled with delight, her phone pressed against the window, taking picture after picture. The sense of danger that had been gnawing them was gradually replaced with a flutter of excitement.

Carson was relieved when they finally checked into the luxury hotel. They even had their own rooms. Hyo said that most of the teams were staying here, in case they wanted to meet the others before the competition. But Carson wasn't tempted to leave his room: if the Logan46 team were here too, he was in no mood for a confrontation. Vanta had assured him that she had altered the hotel records, so any agents watching out for them would think they were part of the Brazilian team.

Instead, Carson sat in his room and set Vanta up for an all-night charge on the bed. She sighed, as if slipping into a hot bath.

"Ah, 220 volts. Makes a nice change from the 240 I was drinking up back home. That went straight to my head! It was just a tad too strong."

"Glad you're enjoying it." He ordered a burger and fries from room service, then ate while he and Vanta watched YouTube videos of the other international racers they'd be competing against tomorrow.

"They're good." Carson yawned as exhaustion washed over him. "Some of them are well better than me."

"I don't know about that," Vanta said. "But I know they're not better than me." She turned to look at Carson, expecting a laugh. But jet lag had got the better of him and he was flat-out, asleep.

The next morning, Carson left Vanta recharging, but could see she was already her usual perky self. He headed down for breakfast in the hotel restaurant with the rest of the Carsonators.

The room was packed with people from across the world – South African, German, Australian, American, and Brazilian were just a few of the accents they caught. They were all fellow racers who eyed one another with a mixture of respect and caution.

They sat in a corner booth. Kay had grunted "Morning. . ." without looking up from her phone. Carson, Trix and Eddie tried to keep to keep a low profile, which was not easy, as Eddie had discovered it was an all-you-can-eat buffet. He returned to their table with his third plate stacked with American pancakes smothered in maple syrup.

"Look at that!" He indicated to his plate like a showman showing off a rare diamond. "I took them *all* and nobody stopped me!"

As he tucked into the food, Carson and Trix noticed people looking their way with curious expressions. They would stare, then quickly talk amongst themselves.

"I think we've been recognized," Trix muttered from behind a spoonful of cereal. Her point was underlined when several teams started to take covert pictures of their table with their mobile phones.

Carson tried to ignore them, but they were fast becoming the centre of attention. Eventually four Chinese young men crossed over to them, staring in fascination.

"Excuse us," their leader said with a smile fixed on his face. "Are you the Carsonators?"

Carson blushed, feeling uncomfortable with the attention. He gave a small nod, which only seemed to please the Chinese team, who exchanged excited comments in Mandarin.

"It's an honour to meet you. Nobody thought you were coming! May we get a selfie?"

Before Carson could object, the team huddled around them and began taking pictures. Within moments other teams approached them asking for selfies too. Kay was edged out of the picture to the side, and watched with increasing astonishment as her brother became a celebrity before her very eyes.

Eventually a familiar face appeared from the crowd and gave a little wave. It was India.

"You finally made it. I was beginning to think getting on a plane was a little too advanced for you."

Carson pulled a face. "Ha, ha. You're hysterical." He tried not to show it, but he was happy to see her. She jerked a thumb towards the other teams.

"You've all become something of a legend here. Not turning up on time made you all mysterious and it turns out you posted the second fastest time in all the regional finals."

Eddie was offended. "Who beat us?"

India lowered her voice. "The Russians. By two seconds." She tilted her head towards their table.

Carson glanced over, noticing they were one of the few teams who hadn't come over to congratulate them. Carson lowered his voice too. "No offense, but why are you here? Didn't you come third?"

India clutched her heart as if she had been stabbed and wailed theatrically. "Ow! So cruel." Then she gave him a playful scowl. "Only *just* third. In the world championships the first heat is for the world's third-place losers, like me. The winning two go to the second heat – all the second-place losers. And the winning two from that. . ."

"Get to race with us kings—" Carson felt Trix kick

him under the table. "And queens," he quickly added.

"Exactly, hot shot. Watch your back." She extended two fingers and pointed to her eyes – then swivelled them around to indicate she would be watching him.

Carson grinned and duplicated the gesture as she disappeared back to her table. It took a moment for him to realize Kay was staring at him with one eyebrow raised.

"What?" said Carson, his cheeks burning as he focused on his breakfast.

Kay dropped the bombshell as they crossed the lobby to meet Hyo.

"I'm coming with you to check all this drone stuff out."

Eddie was horrified. "You're what now?" He noticed the smile she flashed towards the dashing American team pilot. "You can't come."

"Sure I can. After all, I can't let my little brother enjoy all of this attention without me. You're a minor celebrity now! Emphasis on *minor*."

Eddie, Trix and Carson exchanged troubled looks, but couldn't think of anything to put her off.

Hyo was energetically bouncing from one foot to the other as she met them in the lobby. She kept touching her ear as she talked.

"Good morning, Carsonators! Yes, we're in position. I hope you had a good night's sleep? We're on our way and they wanted bottles of shampoo. Is there anything you need?"

"Um . . . it was all good," said Carson. "We're ready."

Hyo smiled enthusiastically. "Their toilet is blocked!"

Carson assumed that was directed to her headset.

"Let's go!"

It took them a moment to realize she was talking to them. Hyo marshalled them through the revolving doors and outside, straight into a mob of reporters. Camera flashes went off and microphones with TV logos from around the world were thrust towards them. The questions came thick and fast.

"Carsonators! As the youngest competitors, do you think you stand a chance against the other teams? How do you like Seoul? What made you want to race drones?"

The trio reeled off a few short answers: "Of course! Brilliant! I was rubbish at football. . ." before

Hyo led them to a private car and they bundled inside – except Kay, who took her time, making the most of the limelight, before Eddie finally yanked her into the vehicle and they headed to the stadium.

As they approached, they could see enormous Contractor League banners hanging all over it, welcoming people in many languages. It certainly looked more impressive than any league event they had seen so far. Kay documented everything on her mobile phone's camera.

"It looks big," said Trix with her face pressed against the window.

Hyo clapped her hands. "It's huge! We are expecting thirty thousand people to attend, and it will be shown on sports channels and online all around the globe! As Mr Marcus Nation says, this is the dawn of a new international sport!"

"Sorry, how many?" Eddie asked, convinced he'd misheard her.

"Thirty thousand!"

Carson swapped alarmed looks with his friends.

"So much for pretending we're not here," he muttered ominously.

Chapter 27
AND THEY BEGIN...

On arrival, Hyo took them directly to the racing paddock under the stadium so they could set up. Kay had been less than impressed with the grungy, garage-like atmosphere, so Hyo arranged a VIP booth so she could watch the games in comfort.

The Carsonators were given the opportunity to do a sight lap, as everybody else had practised the day before. The course was bigger and trickier than the UK final, and the air was more humid, so Carson soon found that his VR headset kept fogging up.

Marcus Nation bounded over in his trademark

Hawaiian shirt. As ever, he was brimming with enthusiasm.

"Carsonators! I'm so happy you made it. We were all beginning to worry." He laughed jovially. "In fact, we'd promised to bump Logan46 into the finals to represent the UK if you didn't come, but here you are!"

Another reason for Logan46 to hate us, thought Carson. Outwardly he nodded and smiled.

"As if we'd miss this."

"Well, best of luck. And watch out for those Russians. They're flying Sledgehammer and have been top of all the racing leagues. They destroyed their competition back in Russia – I mean literally ground their rivals to dust. And they're boasting about how they're going to take you down. They're full of surprises." He winked and walked away.

"He's always such a ray of sunshine," snarked Trix.

The noise from the growing crowds was a dull, rumbling roar as it reverberated in the hall beneath the stadium where all the teams had been assembled. Flags from the competing teams hung from poles mounted to the workbenches.

As usual, the Carsonators had nothing to do before the race, so they placed Vanta on the bench and sat with their feet up, watching, as people frantically ran to and fro around them, seeking replacement parts and attempting last-minute changes to their drones.

On the bench closest to them, they watched as the Japanese entry, Shuriken, was tuned up. Trix studied the drone's unusual star-shaped body and spotted that the edges were razor sharp – and could spin at high speed, like a throwing star.

"Not such a secret weapon," she said, pointing it out to Carson.

Eddie took the time to read the championship race rules. As India had explained to them, each heat would consist of ten laps.

"There's some new rules here. There are green hoops on the course. Failure to pass through them means we're hit with a three-second time penalty. Got that?"

Carson nodded, although he didn't like the idea of piling more rules on top of navigating what was already a complicated course. Eddie continued reading.

"They also encourage racers to arm their drones with *ingenious and devastating weapons*." He looked up from the iPad and gave Vanta a thumbs up. "I think we might have that covered."

The little drone responded by extending the small rocket pod hidden in her belly. The same one that had helped Carson escape through the shopping-centre roof.

"Put that away," said Carson. "Let's try and win this without blowing everybody up."

"Killjoy," Trix mumbled as Hyo enthusiastically bounded over, carrying a parcel.

"Ms Trix, this arrived for you!" Hyo handed it over. "Straight from Japan!" She pointed at the stamps on it.

"You have fan mail?" Eddie asked, with a trace of jealousy.

Trix tore open the packaging. "No. I ordered something online for us, but I wasn't sure whether it would arrive in time." She lifted a plain cardboard box out of the parcel and set about opening that. She then pulled out a pair of VR goggles that looked very different from the ones Carson usually wore. Instead of sliding a phone inside to act as the screen, there was a curved glass screen already built into the headset.

"Ta-da!" Trix handed the goggles to Carson. "These are custom-built according to my specifications, the best I could buy with the prize money we had left." She reached out and tapped the screen. "This is super high-definition, far better than our phones. It should cut down on motion sickness and not strain your eyes, keeping you more focused."

"You are the best!" Carson said, examining them.

Trix pointed to the black mesh panels on the side. "These are for airflow. There's no point in sweating yourself into a puddle, especially in this climate. The speakers are built into the side of the headset, and I've added a microphone so you can easily communicate with us all. It connects to your phone for better coverage."

Hyo gave a giggle of appreciation, then her hand shot to her ever-present earpiece and she listened intently. Then she waved at the team. "See you later! Good luck!" and she walked briskly away, presumably having been called to address another situation.

Carson lifted the goggles over his head and pulled them down to rest on his forehead. "Listen.

I was thinking. Maybe we should split the laps. . ."

Trix wagged her finger. "No way. I won the last race because you gave me a great idea. Without that, we would have been third. You and Vanta are the perfect team here. This is the world championship. This is your race, Carson."

"*Our* race." He fist-bumped her.

All the teams headed to the edge of the pitch for the start of the event. It was already twilight and the enormous arena was filled with neon, smoke and blazing lights. The thirty-thousand-strong crowd only filled half the stadium but made up for it in noise. There were no empty seats, though, as the race course filled not only the pitch, but extended to the end seating areas, cutting the arena in half to make full use of the space. Jumbo video screens were angled everywhere to capture the action from dozens of video cameras. They even had cameras mounted on drones to capture footage from the heart of the race.

The team's racing platform was a stage extended out into the arena. The view was blocked by obstacles dotted around the racecourse, which meant Trix could only be a useful co-pilot over half the course.

The area was separated from the grandstand by security gates that only opened when they pressed their badges against a sensor. The door behind them led straight back to the racing paddock under the stadium.

Carson watched the third-place teams assemble on the edge of the course, and India stood out, with her red hair. She didn't look his way or at the massive crowds; she was focusing all attention on Sixtus. Even from this distance, Carson could see that she had made some modifications, including covers that protected the drone's propellers.

Marcus Nation gave a warm-up speech as the drones took to the air for the hot lap, keeping in perfect formation so the crowd could appreciate them. Carson had planned to pay attention so he could learn from these racers where the real perils lay, but he felt a jab in his arm. He turned around, straight into the angry Logan46 team.

"You stole our place in the final heat!" growled Logan.

"How can we steal something that was ours to begin with?" asked Carson, who, after events over the last few days, couldn't care less about his rival's bullying. "You were second-place losers, Logan. And you were lucky to get that!"

Logan blinked in surprised, clearly not used to anybody talking back to him.

Before he could say anything, Carson continued. "I will be cheering you on to win your heat, just so I can blow you off the track all over again!"

Logan scowled but was lost for any comeback. Other teams nearby had caught the exchange and started to chuckle. Furious, Logan and his team stormed away.

The feelings of anger quickly vanished when the other racers nodded at Carson and threw him thumbs up. Rippling with newfound confidence, Carson turned back to the track just as the first-heat drones sped over the line and the race began in earnest.

With everybody outside, Vanta found herself alone. She hopped around, looking at her rivals, who sat motionless on the tables. The only noise came from the muffled sounds of the stadium above.

"Hello?" she said. Nothing stirred. She regarded her rivals sadly. "So that's what life would be like if I were deleted or if I ran out of power? Nothing more than bolts and circuits. . ."

The sound of approaching footsteps made her lapse into silence. Somebody had entered the paddock and was slowly walking between the tables as if searching for something. Then familiar voices. . .

"It's over here!"

Logan and his cronies hurried over the Vanta. One of them already had a screwdriver in his hand.

"If the damage is subtle, there's no way they'll work out what's wrong with it."

The screwdriver loomed closer to Vanta. Carson had been strict about her not giving away her secret in public, but right now she felt she didn't have a choice as the cold metal of the screwdriver pressed against her engine cowl.

"Hey! What're you doing?"

Team Logan froze, caught in the act of sabotage. Vanta was facing the wrong way, and her rear cameras were blocked by the workbench wall, but she heard several people run over as Logan hastily moved away with his hands raised.

"Nothing! I just noticed this isn't our drone. Silly me. I—"

Whatever he wanted to say next came out in a gasp as a Taser hit him in the chest and he tumbled to the floor from the electric shock pumping through him. His two pals only made it a few steps backwards before they were similarly struck down, writhing on the floor.

Vanta had assumed her saviours were stadium security guards, but her hopes were dashed when Agent Bevan stepped into view, staring at her with a gleam in his eye.

"I know it's you, AG-421 Vanta Hawk. We analysed the race footage carefully. Smaller, but still the same."

He hit a switch on the Taser and the wires retracted back into the weapon. With a low hum it recharged. He aimed the Taser at Vanta. With a sudden silent spin of her rotors, the drone hopped backwards on to another team's adjacent bench, her cameras scanning left and right at the tools around her.

Bevan strode forward. "You're not going anywhere. It's time I put you to sleep."

Vanta suddenly surged sideways at full speed – knocking a soldering iron forward from the bench with such precision that it arced to the floor and struck the man's shin. There was a loud hissing noise as the hot tip burned through his trouser leg and scorched the skin beneath.

He howled and as he hopped aside, his finger squeezed the trigger. The Taser darts shot out and embedded themselves harmlessly into the bench.

Without thinking, Agent Bevan tried to adjust his aim as Vanta zipped off the table, but the Taser wires pulled taut, yanking the weapon from his hand. Bevan tried to scramble after it – in doing so he took his eyes off the drone – which was a terrible mistake.

Vanta had already begun zooming towards him, and she rammed her propellers into his fat fingers. She could still hear him howling as she raced from the room.

Chapter 28
CLOSING IN

Carson punched the air with delight as Sixtus shot across the finishing line in second place.

"That means India is through to the second heat!"

"Whoop-de-doo," Trix replied flatly. "You should be more concerned about *our* race." A frown crossed her face as she looked past Carson. He turned to see what was going on – just as Vanta gently landed in his arms.

"What's going on?" he said before realizing the other racers were giving him peculiar looks. Carson quickly faked a laugh and hurried away from the others. "Oh, very funny!" he shouted to nobody in particular. Everybody's attention drifted back to the race, assuming Vanta's flight was just a silly prank. Trix and Eddie hurried after him, heading down the tunnel that led to the paddock.

"What're you doing?" he hissed at Vanta.

"They're here!"

Carson looked up at the flurry of footsteps as Agent Anders and Bevan appeared at the other end of the tunnel. Bevan was sucking his fingers. He pointed directly at Carson.

"Stop right there!"

Without hesitation, Carson turned and ran. "Come on!"

Trix and Eddie didn't need to be told twice. They pelted through the viewing area as the first-heat teams returned, crossing with the second-heat racers who were preparing to step on to the field. The extra confusion was just what they needed. The milling crowds slowed the agents down just enough for Carson, Trix and Eddie to reach the security gate that led into the main grandstand.

"The controller is still on the bench," Carson suddenly exclaimed as he pressed his security card against the gate's sensor. The gate beeped and they tumbled out into the grandstand just as the stadium began cheering and clapping: the second-heat contestants were taking their places on the launch pads.

"You don't need it! And you have them!" Trix gestured towards the goggles around his neck.

"If we're not controlling Vanta, we can't race," Carson stated, much to Eddie's surprise. "You were right," he added. "And my mum would agree with you too."

Trix considered arguing, but what was the point. She sighed. "Eddie and I'll get the controller! Meet us under that support tower!" She pointed to a concrete post halfway around the stadium, poking from the top tier of the grandstand. It stretched higher to support the roof.

Carson nodded, then sprinted up the steps while the other two ran down the steep incline.

Behind them, Bevan emerged from the paddock. He quickly looked between his targets and chose Carson to pursue.

The steep steps were already causing Carson to fight for breath. He stumbled as he misjudged the edge of one, falling to his hands and knees – dropping Vanta as he fell. The drone took straight to the air and hovered around his shoulder.

"Hurry!" she urged Carson.

The people around them saw what was going on and assumed it was part of the show.

Agent Bevan reached into his jacket for his Taser but didn't dare draw it out in front of so many cameras and witnesses. His indecision was enough for Vanta to arc down at speed and clip him under the chin with her main body in what would have been a perfect right hook. The man was lifted from his feet as he flipped backwards – landing on two other men in black bomber jackets who had been following close behind. The three of them tumbled down the steps.

Carson pushed himself back up and sprang up five more steps, his leg muscles aching with each bound. Then he found himself midway up the grandstand, on a level walkway that circled the stadium. He ran for his life as Vanta caught up with him.

Down below, in the stadium, Marcus Nation announced the second-heat hot lap was about to start.

*

Trix and Eddie sprinted in a long circle at the edge of the pitch, turning back towards another entrance to the team paddock. A security door blocked their path. Pressing their pass cards against the scanner, it opened and they entered a concrete passage. They checked the agents weren't following them before slamming it shut.

The passage led back to the workshop, which was now filled with the first-heat teams dismantling their drones. Trix led the way back to their bench and almost punched the person who leapt in front of her path.

"Whoa! It's me!" exclaimed India as Trix raised her arm.

"Sorry!" Luckily Trix pulled her punch in time. "You just startled me."

India looked around. "Is Carson with you?"

"He's busy." Trix tried to step past her, but India moved to block her path.

"Did you hear? I was second! That means I will be flying against you in the final heat!"

Trix patted her on the shoulder and then pushed past. "Well done."

India looked bewildered as Eddie nudged past,

giving her the thumbs up. "We look forward to you making second again!"

Trix slid to a halt at their bench. Her bag was still there. A quick check assured her that the remote control unit and her iPad were safely inside. She slung the bag around her shoulder as Eddie caught up. He was staring at his phone.

She patted the bag. "Let's go!"

Eddie's eyes didn't move from his phone. Trix nudged him.

"Will you look at that later? We need to go. *Edward?*"

Eddie looked up, his eyes as wide as saucers. "Things just got more complicated." He held up his phone for Trix to see. In disbelief she snatched it off him for a better look.

"Oh, this is bad. . ." she muttered.

"And it's going to get a lot worse," came a voice from behind.

They spun around to see Agent Anders pointing her Taser straight at them.

Chapter 29
HOSTAGE

Running along the walkway made Carson an open target, so he shuffled up several more steps and lost himself in the crowd as Bevan and the others finally resumed the chase.

"And they're off!" yelled Marcus Nation as the second-heat drones began to race.

Carson hunkered down next to a tunnel opening leading inside the grandstand. Vanta sat on his shoulder. From there they could look down on the agents as they searched for them, fruitlessly. The stands were plunged into darkness, save the occasional searchlight artistically drifting over them, so it was unlikely they'd be spotted.

Vanta gave a little hacker face. "I've found the plans for the stadium." She took to the air. "Follow me!" She zipped into the tunnel. Carson gave the agents one last look before following her.

The warren of whitewashed concrete tunnels formed a continuous loop around the stadium, past numerous toilets and snack stands and exits to the car park. A few stragglers were hurrying back to their seats while others impatiently bought drinks, desperate to get back to watch the race. A few of the merchants and spectators watched quizzically as a small drone whizzed past, with Carson sprinting after it – shouting to each other.

"This way," Vanta encouraged him. "We're almost at the bottom of the light tower."

"Do you think the others are there yet?"

"They won't be too far behind, I'm sure."

Like a ripple in a pond, the racers in the workshop all began to take notice of what was happening with Agent Anders. They could all see the Taser pointing at Trix and Eddie. Another two agents, dressed in matching black bomber jackets and caps, joined her.

"Agent Bevan is pursuing the boy," one reported.

Anders shot a thin smile at Eddie and Trix. "See? You're not getting away from us this time." She became aware of the sudden silence around them. Everybody was watching closely. "Go back about your business," she snapped at them. "This doesn't concern you."

None of the racers moved.

"I don't think you're going to shoot us in front of all these people." Trix sounded more confident than she felt. She defiantly pulled her bag further up her shoulder.

"Don't test me, young lady." Agent Anders was rapidly losing patience.

Trix turned to address the racers. "These people are trying to clip our wings. Trying to stop us from racing. Are we going to let them?" She was encouraged by the murmurs of defiance around the room. Trix was warming to her speech and raised her fist high. "The skies belong to us, not them!" The crowd cheered their approval.

As Eddie watched he leaned against the

workbench in apparent defeat while his arm slowly stretched for a box of spanners.

Trix looked around, encouraged by the support. She gave a half-smile and raised an eyebrow. "See you later, Special Agent Loser."

Trix turned to walk away. With a snarl of anger, Anders aimed her Taser.

Eddie hurled the spanners at Agent Anders – knocking the Taser aside as she squeezed the trigger. The Taser darts shot out and electrocuted the grinning agent next to her.

"Why you little—" She didn't get to the end of her sentence as a large drone swooped over the crowd and struck her on the side of the head. It was Sixtus!

"Don't just stand there! Run!" India yelled at them.

The racers all burst into a wild cheer, parting as Trix and Eddie sprinted through them, only to bunch back together to hamper Agent Anders and her remaining sidekick.

Carson and Vanta looked around the foot of the support pole. There was no sign of his friends. The crowd around them burst into applause and got to their feet to celebrate the violent destruction of three drones in a spectacular collision. Carson glanced at the replay on the screen but couldn't tell who had been knocked out, but the lap count caught his eye.

"Carson!" He spun around to see Eddie and Trix sprinting towards him like their lives depended on it.

"Did you get it? We don't have much time before our heat starts."

Eddie waved his hand to shut him up. "They've got... They've got..." He was too out of breath to form words.

Trix snatched Eddie's phone and passed it to Carson. It was open on a message: *Give up, or else...* and beneath it was a photograph of Kay, held by a menacing-looking agent. Carson couldn't tell where it had been taken, exactly, but it must have been somewhere inside the stadium, as they could just see the racetrack behind her.

"Oh no ... she was sent to the VIP booth. Anybody know which one? I haven't seen Hyo around..."

Vanta hovered over his shoulder to see the picture. "I can triangulate her position using the stadium map ... got it." She spun to face the grandstand opposite. "That picture was taken from the booths over there. Although it's too difficult to identify exactly which one."

"As long as they don't have Vanta, they won't harm her," said Trix slowly. "If she's racing, they'll think we're all in the racing paddock." She glanced at Eddie. "Which means they'll rush over, while Eddie and I can go and rescue Kay while they're distracted."

Eddie looked confused. "But if they find Carson standing down there —" he pointed to the pitch "— they'll just arrest him on sight. Then it's game over anyway!"

Carson nodded. "You're right. So I won't stand down there. I'll get a bird's-eye view of the race instead, and give them a real distraction."

They followed his gaze up the support column. A metal ladder was bolted all the way up to an access hatch in the angular roof above them.

"Aren't you supposed to pilot the drone from the paddock?" Eddie asked.

Carson shrugged. "I don't remember reading that in the rules."

Trix shook her head as she peered upwards. "It's a long way up. We could just let Vanta race on her own..."

Carson shook his head and smiled. "That's not really the point, is it? Kay is being held hostage and that's our fault. All we're racing for now is to cause a distraction, so I'll keep them busy trying to reach me while you two save her."

Trix nodded. "We better get a move on if we're going to do this. Stay in touch using our phones."

"I'll patch us together on a shared call," said Vanta. Moments later their phones all gave a short ring, then automatically connected. "There."

Eddie was impressed. "Is there anything you can't do?"

"I've always wanted to juggle."

As if on cue, the stadium burst into wild cheering: the second heat had just finished.

"Let's go, team!" With that, Vanta zoomed over the spectators and headed for the pitch.

Trix gave Carson a hug. "Try not to fall."

Eddie offered a fist bump. "Try not to lose."

Trix and Eddie hurried into the darkness of the grandstand.

Carson took a deep breath, checked nobody was watching, then began to climb the narrow ladder. He judged he had already climbed the equivalent of two storeys and his arms when his legs started trembling from exhaustion. He had at least five more to go.

"Don't look down," he mumbled to himself. He wasn't afraid of heights, but clinging to a ladder at the top of a stadium was probably something he thought he should be afraid of. He stopped and caught his breath, looping his forearm through the rung for extra security.

The ladder was mounted at the back of the concrete support, which meant the crowd couldn't see him, but it also meant he couldn't see the pitch.

Marcus Nation's voice washed over him. "Spain's Conquistadors won that heat, so they will join our champions in the grand final. And second place, almost making it through by the narrowest of margins . . . it's the UK's Logan46! Check them out, they look like they've had a bit of a shock recently!"

The very mention of their name washed away any fatigue Carson was feeling. With a grunt of effort, he continued his climb. . .

Chapter 30
SEARCH AND DESTORY

Eddie was out of breath as he jogged behind Trix. They had decided there was little point in hiding in the shadows, so took to running around the walkway, confident that they were unlikely to be seen in the dark, shadowy lighting scheme.

"Let's cut down here," said Trix. She turned into the tunnel that led under the grandstand – then suddenly shuffled to a halt and pushed Eddie to the side. "I don't think he saw us!" she hissed.

Eddie craned around her to see what the problem was. At the end of the tunnel was a hot dog stall with a black-jacketed agent leaning on the counter making an order. He had his back to them for the moment, but all he had to do was turn around and they would be found.

"Maybe we could go the other way around?" Eddie glanced across the arena: it was a *long* way, and they might still face the same problem.

"And we're on to the final race!" boomed Marcus Nation's voice. "Champions from across the world will be joined by our gold star winners from heats one and two!"

Trix looked up at the video screens as Nation started to list the competitors, accompanied by pounding rock music. Pictures of the teams and their drones appeared in succession, with each nation's flag draped in the corner. She saw the Carsonators up there, the photos taken from outside the hotel, showing them looking confused.

"We don't have much choice," she said. Eddie followed her gaze across the section of the racetrack that lay ahead of them. "We're going to have to go over that. . ."

Carson shouldered the roof hatch as hard as he could, but it remained stubbornly closed.

Reaching the top of the ladder, his arms and legs were numb from the effort. He wrapped both arms around the top rung and peered down. The darkness of the grandstand disguised how far he was above the people. About eight stories, he guessed. He doubted he had the strength to hold on for the climb down; falling was a terminal option.

He closed his eyes and held on as Marcus Nation drew the crowd's attention to the racers gathering at the launch pad.

"And there's the Carsonators' drone ready for action ... but wait! I don't see the team at all. Where's the pilot?"

"Stuck up a stupid ladder," grumbled Carson. He heard the reaction from the audience and could imagine the spotlights moving over the stadium to try and find him.

Nation faltered as he continued. "Well ... they're not where they should be ... but they're obviously flying the drone from *somewhere*. There's no rule saying they must pilot it from there..." There was a loud thump as Nation's hand covered the microphone, but his obscured voice could still be heard across the stadium as he consulted with his officials. "There isn't, is there?" He received his answer and uncovered the mic, speaking with renewed enthusiasm. "No, there's apparently not! So wherever the camera-shy Carsonators are hiding . . . get ready!"

Carson could hear the drones take flight for the hot lap. If he couldn't take control of Vanta before the race began properly then he knew she would launch herself; he didn't mind for the hot lap, but he wanted control once the race began. He wanted to win fair and square. He wanted to win it for his mum.

And now for his dad.

With a grunt he pushed against the metal hatch with all his might. The rusty hinges gave a squeal and it flipped open. Carson lost no time scrambling through, then closed it, looping his belt through a hook to prevent it from being opened from below. The roof circled the stadium in a series of crested waves made from white metal panels that were covered in a thick layer of city grime. Not that he cared. He lay on his back to catch his breath, while turning on the VR visor hanging around his neck.

"Can you all hear me?"

"Carson! Where are you?" asked Vanta. "We're almost halfway around the hot lap!"

"Give me a second and I'll be in position." He rolled over and moved on his hands and knees towards the edge of the roof. He had a breathtaking view of the arena. He sat on the edge, feet dangling over the crowd far below, and slipped the headset on. "Visor's on."

He felt a sudden disorientation as Vanta's point of view filled his vision, which wasn't a pleasant feeling, sitting on the edge of a roof. But Trix had been right: the high-definition screen made a huge difference.

He reached into his bag and took the remote control unit out. He didn't need to see to find the power switch.

"Connection established," Vanta informed him. "Welcome aboard, captain!"

"Thank you. Now, we have a race to win. Trix, Eddie, where are you?"

There was a pause before Eddie spoke, sounding somewhat on edge. "Er, we had a little problem we're sorting out. . ."

*

Lying on their bellies, Trix and Eddie commando-crawled along the end of the stadium. The seats had all been removed and replaced with a forest of metal poles that stretched different heights, up to seven metres tall. The tops of them spewed fountains of multicoloured sparks designed to confuse the racers as they weaved their way through.

"I can't talk right now," said Eddie into his phone, which was poking from his pocket. He could feel the sting of hot embers as they spat down on them. Then, with a terrible whine, the drones suddenly rushed overhead like a flock of electric bats. Most stayed high, but several avoided the sparks by dropping low and narrowly passing over Trix and Eddie – forcing them to sprawl flat against the floor. The drones were moving too fast for the pilots to be able to spot two figures crawling the darkness below.

Within seconds the racers had passed. Luckily the curtain of sparks and the safety barriers put up at the edge of the track had kept them obscured from the crowd and cameras.

"Hurry!" shouted Trix as she resumed scrambling forward and hissing in pain as the occasional spark sizzled her scalp. "I don't want to be here when they come around again!"

They rushed towards the barrier that would see them back into the stadium proper. Then Eddie suddenly stopped Trix and pushed her low into the shadows. Four agents were standing just beyond the barrier, each pressing one hand to their earpieces as they searched around for any sign of the Carsonators.

Eddie felt his heart in his mouth. They hadn't been seen yet . . . but it was just a matter of time.

Carson was experiencing an odd moment of calm despite the peril they were all in. When he guided Vanta through the forest of sparks it felt as if he were really there and not sitting on the edge of the roof. Maybe it was the new VR goggles, or the fact he had ridden on top of Vanta and felt the wind in his face; whatever it was, he now felt as if he and Vanta had become one. Boy and machine working in perfect harmony.

"When we passed the VIP boxes I was able to take surveillance footage," said Vanta as a small window superimposed to the side of Carson's main vision. The video played a frame at a time and, while it was blurry due to the speed, Carson could make out a scared-looking Kay standing at the window with a pair of agents guarding her from behind. "I'll send this to Eddie's phone."

"Eddie, did you hear that?" said Carson as he zigzagged Vanta through a series of curving pipes that ended in a dizzying helter-skelter.

Eddie's reply came as a subdued whisper. "Yes. But we're a little stuck right now. We could sure do with a distraction."

"I'm a little busy," said Carson as the drones emerged close to the ground where a series of giant mechanical hammers thudded from side to side. Moving at half speed in the hot lap, they were easy to avoid. Carson doubted they would be so easy at full speed.

"Next time, remember they'll move in the same sequence," Vanta told him. "Just like the first race."

Carson recalled how the moving slabs in the race had moved in a repeated pattern as the mechanical motors turned. He could see a similar repetition here. "Got it."

Clear of that hazard, he lined Vanta up for the start line that was looming ahead. The moment they crossed it the hot lap would be over, and the real race would begin.

"Eddie, get ready for your distraction," Vanta said, as cool as ever.

Then Marcus Nation's voice boomed across the stadium. "Here we go! For the title of world champion... GET SET – *RACE!*"

At that moment, the drones shot over the start line and one of the automated spotlights suddenly swivelled around and picked out Carson perched on the edge of the roof.

Marcus Nation's voice suddenly yelled out in astonishment. "Well, it looks like we found the Carsonators, folks. But what the heck is he doing up there?"

Every eye in the stadium was torn between watching the drones and looking up at Carson. He didn't need to see any of this to know he had been found.

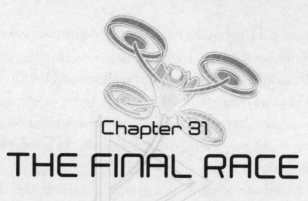

Chapter 31
THE FINAL RACE

Eddie and Trix heard the gasps from the crowd following Marcus Nation's announcement. Only when the four agents ran away did they see where they were heading. Carson was clearly illuminated by the single spotlight, his feet dangling over the edge of the roof.

"Thanks for the distraction, Vanta," said Eddie. "But, Carson, you better watch it. The agents know where you are!"

This time there was no hesitation as Vanta crossed the line ending the hot lap. Her engines spooled faster and she powered forward. Within moments she was vying for the lead between the Russians' Sledgehammer and the Japanese Shuriken.

Carson heard Eddie's warning, but it didn't worry him. No matter what, their adventure would come to an end tonight, and he would rather go out in a blaze of glory than give up now. A quick check in the rear monitor made him smile. Logan46 was several places back and being overtaken by Sixtus.

"Get ready!"

Vanta's warning drew his attention back to the first obstacle, a series of hoops the drones had to pass through. Missing any would incur a time penalty.

"Piece of cake!" Carson said, recalling them from the sighting lap. Back then he wondered why the league was using such basic obstacles.

Then the hoops began to move, some bobbing up and down, others left and right. The hoops were drones themselves! This hadn't happened on the sight lap or during the previous two heats, and from the crowd's reaction he could tell it was a surprise for them too.

It forced the racers to quickly change direction

as one. The leaders bunched together like a shoal of fish as they swooped through one hoop, then all sharply lifted up for the next moving target.

Sledgehammer suddenly veered towards Vanta in an attempt to knock her away from the hoop. Carson slammed on the air brakes and they fell behind as the Russian overshot and struck the Canadian drone, which spun sideways, missing passing through the loop completely and causing the time-penalty alarm to sound.

Carson fell in behind Sledgehammer. "So *that's* the kind of game you want to play," he growled.

They passed through the remaining hoops and on to the next obstruction.

Trix and Eddie had finally crawled off the side track and into the opposite grandstand, which was filled with international fans banging drums in support of their team. With the race in full flight and the darkness of the grandstands, nobody paid them any attention. They ran as fast as they could around the stadium walkway, their gaze locked on the VIP boxes ahead, built above the standard seats to offer the perfect view.

Eddie had received Vanta's photo, so they knew which section Kay was being held in. The private box was fairly dark, but he could just make out his sister's pale face looking out at the race.

"She looks scared."

"Do you blame her? I'd be terrified. I *am* terrified! It looks like there's no way inside the boxes from out here."

Eddie pointed to a tunnel entrance, which was guarded by an agent who leaned against a storage cupboard door built into the tunnel wall, his attention on the race. "I reckon that's our way in." The tunnel had seats either side and above it, packed with Korean fans waving banners to support their team.

"How are we going to get past him?" She didn't like the smile forming on Eddie's face. "What?"

The agent watched the race with growing excitement. The drones were slaloming through a network of moving concrete blocks, some positioned diagonally across their path. He punched the air and gasped – then cheered – with the rest of the stadium as a drone misjudged the opening ahead and exploded as it struck the block.

"Excuse me, mister," said a young black girl with her hair spiked straight up, who shuffled up to him. "I can't find my parents."

The agent turned his attention back to the race. "Go and find security. They're the ones in the bright green coats." He had lost the drones over the track, so followed the action on the jumbo screens.

"But I can't find them either!" wailed the girl.

Irritated, the agent stepped from the tunnel towards her. Whatever he was about to say was knocked from him as something very heavy fell on to his head.

It was Eddie, dropping a packed litter bin from over the tunnel entrance.

It bounced from the agent's head, spilling dozens of empty junk food cartons. He staggered, dazed. He unsteadily groped for his Taser but dropped it as Trix darted past him and opened the storage cupboard door. Eddie shouldered the already unbalanced man towards the cupboard. As he crashed inside, the Taser was flung from his hand. Eddie reached in and managed to snag the man's little earpiece before slamming the door closed and sharply pulling the bar down to lock it securely.

Eddie slid the earpiece in. "Yew! Earwax..." He stooped to pick up the agent's Taser. "Careful with that!" Trix hissed.

"Hey, I'm an ace sharpshooter." To demonstrate, he tried to spin the gun around his finger as he'd seen cowboys do in movies – and promptly dropped the Taser, which clattered loudly on the concrete floor.

Trix placed a finger over her lips, glaring at Eddie for his clumsiness.

The short tunnel led to a T-junction that allowed VIPs to enter their private boxes without being seen by the crowds outside. Trix pressed up against the corner and peeked around. Luckily there were no other guards posted at the door to the box.

She tiptoed towards the door. She could hear two voices from inside, neither of which were Kay's. She looked around for anything that might help them. There was nothing but a red fire extinguisher hooked to the wall. She whispered into her phone.

"Carson, we might need another distraction to get inside."

Carson swung his legs over the edge of the roof. Despite the peril they were all in, he had to admit that he was beginning to enjoy the tournament. It was faster than any of the others had been, with more surprises to overcome. But it was also deadlier, so he tried to force everything from his mind and concentrate on the race, to keep Vanta safe. And the longer he kept the spotlight on him and the distraction going, the more time his friends had for Kay's rescue.

A rattling from the roof access hatch told him that an agent was trying to reach him, but he had faith that his leather belt would keep it shut. Sure enough, it stopped moments later, presumably because the defeated agent had begun his long climb back down.

The racers were just coming to the end of the third lap and already numerous rivals had bitten the dust. The Brazilian team had briefly taken the lead before Sledgehammer had revealed its weaponry and shot a jet of fire at them. In an instant, the Brazilian drone had become an out-of-control fireball that plummeted to the ground with such force it formed a small crater.

Carson was brought back to the moment by Trix's request for help.

"You want *more* of a diversion? I'm a little busy at the moment."

"I have an idea," said Vanta. "Carson, on the turn after the hoops you're going to have to position me as far to the right as possible. Keep as close to the grandstands as you can."

Carson played the course through his head. He should be going left, not right; it would mean wasting time.

"And I want you to ram Sledgehammer. Annoy him. Get him to follow us. It's time we started giving the crowd what they want."

That made Carson smile. "OK. Trix? Get ready, we're entering that stretch now."

With the hoops ahead, Vanta moved in position just behind and under Sledgehammer, who was still leading.

"Almost. . ." said Vanta. "Get ready – now!"

Carson jerked the controls and pulled Vanta into an acrobatic flip that clipped Sledgehammer. The big Russian drone hadn't expected the move. It sharply veered to the left – smashing through the side of a hoop. Vanta flipped gracefully overhead towards the outermost hoop and, as expected, Sledgehammer followed.

Vanta's weapon pod flipped open, revealing the

tiny pencil-size missiles within – but she didn't fire immediately.

The pause gave the Russian pilot just enough time to realize what he was looking at.

"Boppers away!" she yelled.

Then she fired.

In panic, Sledgehammer swooped aside, losing speed, and missed passing through the outer hoop. A loud squawk across the arena signalled the Russians had incurred a time penalty. Vanta just managed to make it through the hoop, but her missile fell wide as the Russians evaded it.

Carson piloted Vanta back towards the race pack, but the move had cost them. Seven other racers had taken the lead, including Sixtus and Logan46.

Meanwhile, the fired missile streaked straight for the VIP boxes!

Chapter 32
THE RESCUE!

Inside the VIP box, Kay was frozen to the spot as the missile headed straight towards her.

At the very last second it detonated before it could strike the window. The glass shattered into a cobweb of white fractures – but didn't break. Kay and the two agents guarding her threw themselves to the floor.

At the same time, the door was kicked open with a loud thud and Eddie ran into the room with a whoop, holding the Taser gun at arm's length. The agent nearest him on the floor looked and scowled at him. It was Bevan, his injured fingers now heavily bandaged.

"You!"

Eddie grinned. "Surprise!" With that he pulled the trigger and the darts thudded into Agent Bevan's bum. He shrieked in pain as electricity jolted through him, then he lay in a daze, drooling on the floor.

Seeing Eddie was now unarmed, the second agent started to climb to his feet – only to be sprayed in the face by a jet of foam from the fire extinguisher Trix was wielding as she followed her friend inside.

The agent coughed and spluttered as he clawed the foul-tasting foam from his mouth. He staggered backwards – only to be tripped by Kay. With a wail, the agent plunged through the cracked window frame and on to the crowd underneath in a shower of glass. Kay and Trix ran forward, afraid they'd hurt the man, or worse – but broke into laughter when they saw, despite his kicking and screaming, that he was surfing the crowd like a rock star, being borne away over the heads of the crowd towards the front of the grandstand.

Eddie grinned at his bewildered sister. "Did somebody order a rescue?"

*

Carson's lip was numb as he nervously chewed it. He throttled Vanta forward, overtaking the Australians to make fifth place. Logan46 was just ahead, Sixtus to one side, and Shuriken had taken the lead. He was satisfied to see Sledgehammer even further behind; even if they made up the ground, the time penalty had effectively put them out of the race for now.

He tried to accelerate, but Vanta didn't respond. Frustrated, he slapped the side of his controller.

"Vanta, what's wrong? The controls feel sluggish."

"I'm detecting interference. Somebody's scanning our frequency. I think our little missile stunt has annoyed somebody."

"Can we switch channels?"

"OK. Try now."

Carson was rewarded with a jolt of speed and he followed Logan46 into the seventh lap.

The race was now a game of leapfrog. Vanta overtook Logan46 only for his arch-rivals to slip past as the South African in third place tried to attack Vanta with a flailing whip that extended out on a telescopic arm. Angry sparks crackled down its length.

"Carson!"

"I see it," replied Carson, his voice taut with concentration as he avoided the whip. It narrowly missed both Vanta and Logan46, who were forced to fall back just out of range.

Crossing the line into lap eight, Vanta and Logan46 were now in joint fourth position. The sweeping hammer obstacle took out the South African contender, and Vanta inched into third place.

"Carson, something's coming straight at us."

A quick check behind showed that Sixtus was just behind Logan46.

"That's just India."

"No, I don't mean in the race."

Carson felt the wind around him pick up with a roar, and he was suddenly very aware of the danger of being blown off the roof. As they reached a racing straight to start lap nine, he pulled his goggles half up to see what was going on.

A midnight-black helicopter rose from behind the stadium, causing the fierce breeze. From below, the crowd probably thought it was a part of the TV coverage, as news choppers had been circling the stadium all evening.

The chopper's side door slid back, revealing a scowling Agent Anders.

"Carson, what's going on?" Vanta shouted in his ear.

"They've found a way to get up here!" Carson exclaimed, leaping to his feet. With the goggles half covering his eyes, he started to run.

"Carson! There's no escape, kid!" yelled Anders. She jumped the metre from the aircraft to the roof and gave chase.

The roof sloped up, then down, then up again in a series of undulating waves that made Carson's leg muscles tremble with exertion. He angled the VR visor so one eye could see the screen, the other to make sure he didn't run off the edge of the roof.

"I'm coming!" said Vanta urgently.

Carson felt her take control. "NO! We finish the race!"

Vanta didn't argue as Carson seized back control and accelerated the drone with all the power he could muster. The crowd went wild as Vanta focused on the American drone in front, the Eagle, which was just behind Shuriken.

Running while trying to pilot the drone was an

almost impossible task. His feet slipped on the metal slopes and he kept falling to his knees. Luckily, Agent Anders wasn't finding it any easier, as the downwash from the helicopter kept blowing her over.

Carson stumbled and landed on his knees. His thumb accidentally shoved the control sticks. Vanta jerked straight into the Eagle, suddenly moving at full speed. Her military-grade, reinforced fuselage was much stronger than the Americans' lightweight plastic drone, and she tore through the centre of it as if it were an overly ripe melon.

The crowd became louder than ever in their enthusiasm as the Eagle was torn into two halves in a mass of flames and sparks.

"Oh, that's gotta hurt!" Marcus Nation bellowed. "And that puts the Carsonators into second place!"

Carson struggled to his feet, feeling disorientated. He didn't know which way he was facing, or where Agent Anders or the edge of the roof was. He readjusted his goggles so he could see Vanta's view.

"Are you OK?" Carson's thumbs jerked the control sticks to weave Vanta through the array of moving concrete blocks.

"That was unexpected! I'm not indestructible,

you know. Some debris struck my engines, so I had to reroute power. I should be OK."

They zoomed over the line and Marcus Nation declared: "The final lap!"

"Watch out behind!"

In the rear-view, Carson saw that Logan46 had caught up and was on a collision course for Vanta. He impacted her at full speed. Carson felt the jolt through his body – and it took him a split second to realize he had been tackled by Agent Anders. He fell back hard, his VR headset tumbling off. Luckily the controller was in still clutched in his hands. Carson kicked at Anders, pushing her down the slope.

He reached for his helmet – only to see it tumble off the edge of the roof. His free hand checked his phone was still in his pocket, still connected to Vanta.

"I've lost my goggles! I'm flying blind."

"Well, a lot of *left* would help right about now!" Vanta wailed.

Carson jinked the stick to the left. In his mind's eye he could see the section Vanta was approaching. He ran to the edge of the roof and squinted down – he could just see the pack of drones, but from this distance they were nothing more than a bunch of blinking lights.

Then he caught the video feeds on the jumbo screen. He would have to control Vanta using them.

"Vanta, I think you should take over now."

"What? No."

"Vanta! This is crazy."

"Then let's quit the race. There's no harm in doing that. But if you let me fly then Eddie was right all along. We'll be cheats and everyone will know it. It's better to lose now and fly again than to be disqualified for ever from something you love. Think about it. What would your mum want you to do?"

Carson's mind was filled with conflicting emotions. They had got so far and Vanta was right: quitting was the safer option.

On the big screen, he could see parts of Logan46's fuselage were cracked and broken, revealing the electronics beneath. In places it was barely hanging on. They were lining up to ram Vanta again. Clearly their intention was no longer to win, it was to stop the Carsonators from completing the race.

Carson was suddenly yanked backwards as Agent Anders pulled him by the collar.

"Get away from the edge!"

Carson dropped the controller and watched it slide away from him. He lunged for it, pulling himself free from Agent Anders at the precise moment the helicopter hovered closer. The hurricane-force wind helped propel Carson towards the controller. He rolled, then was suddenly sliding headfirst towards the edge.

His outstretched hand caught the controller as it launched into the air – but he couldn't stop himself from plunging over the edge!

His flailing hand caught the rim of the rooftop and he hung from one arm, the controls still in his other hand. The entire stadium erupted in gasps – not regarding him, but because Vanta had just unleashed a missile at Logan46, tearing off the rotors along one side.

Logan46 spun like a Catherine wheel, rapidly losing speed. Sixtus was right behind and pitched to the side – just as Sledgehammer was about to unleash a jet of flame. Then Logan46 collided with the Russians in the largest explosion the games had yet seen. And the crowd loved it!

Carson had missed it all as he hung for his life.

He could just hear Vanta's voice from his phone issuing instructions, which he carried out one-handed on the controller by stretching his index and little fingers across the joysticks. One slip and it would easily fall from his hand.

"Hard left – straighten up . . . down a little. Right. Left – faster!"

He didn't have to look at a screen, not that he could, to imagine how Vanta was cutting through the air. They had become the perfect team, so much so he could fly blindfold and single-handed . . . while dangling for his life.

"Give me your hand, kid!" Agent Anders lay flat on the roof, reaching for him. Her stern expression had melted to one of genuine concern. "This has gone too far! Drop the controller and give me your hand."

Vanta's instructions kept coming. "Right . . . down, quick! Up! That's it Carson – we're almost there!"

"Kid! Drop it or you'll fall!"

Carson could feel his fingers sliding . . . but then the image of his smiling mum came into sharp focus. It was the last time she had ever sat on the end of his bed and read *Around the World in Eighty Days* to him. She adored the fact that the hero, Phileas Fogg, was convinced he had been defeated, but then had pulled victory from the jaws of defeat.

"Let that be a lesson," she had told him. *"Do what you love and try your best. Because best wins every time."*

"Almost there. . ." he heard Vanta say, although her voice now sounded far away. Even Agent Anders' voice now sounded distant, drowned out by the blood pounding in his ears.

Then his fingers gave way, and Carson was suddenly falling.

And all around him the stadium erupted with screams. . .

Chapter 33
REUNION

Trix, Eddie and Kay had been running back around the stadium with one eye on the giant screens. Trix had stopped in her tracks, the others bumping into her, when she saw Carson tumble from the edge of the roof opposite them and hang from one arm.

She pointed, words refusing to escape her dry throat.

"Vanta! Carson's in big trouble!"

Trix flinched as enormous explosions erupted across the stadium. Marcus Nation bellowed that the race had finished and the Constructor League had its first world champion. Trix gathered her senses, realizing that the explosions were celebratory fireworks detonating across the racetrack and high above the stadium.

But she didn't care about that. Her gaze was drawn back to Carson falling to his death!

She blinked against the dazzling pyrotechnics as something shot through them to intercept Carson. A stream of fireworks forced Trix to look away. When she turned back, Carson had disappeared.

Carson must have blacked out. When he woke up he was lying flat on Vanta, who was now the size of a small car. With a screech from her engines she was rapidly plummeting into the stadium car park.

"You caught me. . ." Carson said weakly.

Vanta didn't respond. She banked between rows of parked cars and, a metre from the ground, she suddenly snapped back to her small size and dropped the rest of the way – along with Carson, tumbling several metres along the concrete ground.

For a moment, Carson didn't have the strength to move. He only opened his eyes when the roaring clatter from the helicopter drew closer. Without moving, he watched it land in a set of empty parking bays. He crawled over to Vanta, who was motionless; only a faint light was barely visible in her tail orb.

"Vanta? Vanta . . . are you damaged?"

He scooped up the little drone as Agent Anders rushed from the chopper.

"Kid? Are you OK?"

Carson hugged Vanta protectively. "Get away from me! You can't have her!"

Anders stopped and regarded him with pity.

"She doesn't belong to you, kid. She's dangerous."

"No, she's not. She's my friend."

"—Carson?"

Carson thought he was imagining the new voice. Tears were stinging his eyes as he looked past Anders and, to his astonishment, saw his dad climbing from the helicopter.

"Son. . ."

"Dad? What are you doing here?"

His dad wiped his own tears away. "When I found out my son was in Korea, what do you think I did?" He hesitated as the next words came out as husky croak. He cocked a finger at Agent Anders. "I had to ask the military for a free ride, though." He sniffed away more tears.

"We had to call him," said Anders, almost apologetically. "You fled the country, after all."

"You can't let them have her, Dad." Carson hugged the drone tighter.

Another man exited the chopper and stepped forward.

"Hello, Vanta."

Carson felt the drone tremble in his arms and Vanta illuminated with a weak flickering light. Carson angled her around so she could see the Indian man.

"Father?"

Jira Zushi moved closer, then knelt down so he was level to Carson.

"Hello, Vanta. I missed you."

"I missed you too."

"You have to come back. But this world –" he gestured to the stadium "– it's not for you."

"It is!" snapped Carson. "It's perfect for her! You can't delete her. She's not just a computer ... she's *real*."

"Things are not so simple, Carson. But I want to thank you for looking after her." Jira reached out his hands for Vanta, but Carson held Vanta tighter.

"He's right." Vanta used the last of her power to wriggle to look up at Carson. "I have to go now. All good things come to an end." Her voice weakened. "I'm running on empty. . . I calculate that I'm not going to make it." Even as he watched, the lights within Vanta's orb began to dim. "You can't save me this time, Carson. It's been fun. The best time of my life."

Between his tears and dribbling nose, Carson couldn't find his words. But he didn't resist when Jira gently took Vanta out of his hands.

"I'll never forget you, Carson. Thanks for being my friend."

"Don't go. . ."

The lights in Vanta dimmed . . . then extinguished.

Jira carried the drone back towards the helicopter. Carson's body shook as he sobbed. Then a pair of strong arms embraced him. It was his dad. They hugged for the first time in a long time, and nothing needed to be said.

Eddie, Trix and Kay sprinted across the car park, shouting at the top of their lungs. "Hey! Carson!"

"Hey! We won!" gasped Eddie, breathless with

excitement. He pulled the agent's stolen earpiece from his ear. "I heard the chopper landed here on this thing. . ." He stopped and took in the situation. "What did we miss?"

Chapter 34
THE END OF A SUMMER

Carson hadn't counted the days since they returned. It had helped to take his mind off Vanta that a new school term had started. Eddie had been right: they'd won. The Carsonators were the world champions, Shuriken taking second and the Australians a surprise third, after just pipping Sixtus to the post. India didn't seem to mind, though; she was delighted with fourth.

But the victory didn't mean anything to Carson Lox. Not without Vanta. He couldn't recall a single word from Marcus Nation's rousing speech, and felt no elation when he hoisted the trophy up to the rapturous applause from the stadium.

That night in the hotel, Trix, Eddie and Kay finally called their parents to explain what had happened. Fortunately the agents had done most of that for them, so it only remained for them to apologize and accept the fact they would be grounded for the rest of the summer, if not for ever.

That done, they all gathered in Carson's room. His dad told them that Jira had insisted the military would take no further action against them if they all remained quiet about what had happened with Vanta. Then he insisted they tell him their side of the story. All the way through he nodded encouragingly and never once butted in.

"I don't get it," Carson said, staring at the trophy on the table of the hotel room.

"Don't get what?" his dad asked, picking the trophy up and admiring the way the lights reflected from it.

"Why you're being so . . . calm about all of this. Especially as their parents went bonkers." He nodded towards his friends.

"It's completely understandable that they did. But they're not here." His dad put the award down and stared levelly at his son. His low tone gave nothing away. "Are you all safe and well?" There was a chorus of muted *yeses* from everybody. "Then what's the problem?" Carson opened his mouth to answer, but his dad continued, "And if you want to know the truth, I'm so proud of you."

Carson didn't quite believe what he was hearing.

"You won the world championship. But even that means nothing." He rubbed his stubbled chin as he mustered his thoughts. "When I was your age I always dreamed that I'd get to have such amazing escapades. And you know what? They never happened. But you lot –" he looked at each of them, and they noticed a tear quivering in the corner of his eye "– all of you had the opportunity to be part of something magical. I'm so proud of you all. And a little jealous too," he added with a smile.

To all their surprise, he suddenly burst into laughter. "Your mum and me always got up to high jinks before you were born, of course." He lapsed into silence, shaking his head, lost in memories.

Carson disrupted his musings. "Like. . .?"

"Oh, like the time we drove out to Area 51 in Nevada. You know, the super-secret air force base that everybody knows about? We camped out trying to spot flying saucers."

"And did you see any?" Eddie asked breathlessly.

"Nothing!" Carson's dad burst into laughter so infectious they all started chuckling. "But it was a great night. We managed to scare each other senseless, and security chased us. It was brilliant," he added fondly. "Your mother had a wonderful thirst for adventure." He saw Carson's surprise. "That's why *Around the World in Eighty Days* was her favourite book. That's what I see when I look at you. I see your mum."

Carson blinked a tear away. He was shocked to discover that his dad was so interesting. The rest of the night and the whole flight back home was spent with his dad happily recounting tales of how he and Carson's mum had travelled all over when they were younger. Carson listened with rapt attention; he'd never heard any of the stories before. Nor had he seen his dad so happy.

True to their word, Trix and Eddie donated their share of the prize money to Carson's dad. During Carson's last week of his summer holidays his dad took some rare time off and they went on days out, watched movies together, played computer games and his dad had even started to cook meals — but they were so terrible that Carson pleaded they eat out.

The only thing missing from his life was Vanta.

While it was wonderful to spend time with his dad, he missed Vanta's company, especially the reading of stories before bedtime. She had been a friend he had trusted with his life, and she was just as easy to talk to as his mother had been.

The nights now seemed just as lonely as they had been before.

Returning home from school, Carson wasn't surprised that his dad was still at work. But at least his dad now only had one job, so he would come home earlier than he used to.

Carson sat on his bed and stared at the new racing drone on his desk. It was a top-of-the-line model his dad had bought for him, insisting the Carsonators defend their world title for the next games. Carson knew they'd have to start practising again eventually, but these days he hadn't been able to drum up the enthusiasm; the drone had remained on his desk, un-flown.

There was a clatter from downstairs, and Carson rose to investigate. A courier had crammed a parcel through the letter box. Carson was surprised to discover that it was addressed to him. He took the battered package back up to his room.

Inside the box was a glass sphere. It looked just like the orb that had powered Vanta.

With trembling hands he held it up to the window and examined the fine lines and connectors inside, but it lacked power. Maybe Jira had sent it to him as a keepsake?

No ... that didn't feel right. Even looking at it brought back a wave of painful memories. Why would Jira want to do that to him? There had to be another reason ... but what?

Curious, he held the orb close to the drone on his desk. The glass suddenly lit up as it drew nearer. He could feel the surface of the orb quiver as part of it changed shape, tendrils that looked like chewing gum reached out and bonded with the drone. Then the orb glowed brightly.

Carson took a step back as a noise echoed around his room.

BEE-BOP!

The drone's blades suddenly gave an experimental spin. Then he heard a familiar voice.

"Hello, Carson. Miss me?"